Friends and Vague Lovers

Friends
and Vague Lovers

Jack Dunphy

Farrar, Straus and Young

NEW YORK

To Truman Capote

Would anything but a madman complain of uncertainty? Uncertainty and expectation are the joys of life. Security is an insipid thing, and the overtaking and possessing of a wish, discovers the folly of the chase. Never let us know one another better: for the pleasure of a masquerade is done when we come to show our faces.

LOVE FOR LOVE

PART I: *The Balcony*

[*Chapter One*]

MORE CERTAIN THAN most people that she would not
want to live her life over again, Mrs. Markham had come to
Italy to see to it that she did not try. Wary of repetition, she
rose early and stepped with a singular lack of expectancy
between the long, pale glass doors onto her balcony. She
stood, not as though she had the whole long day to do so
—which indeed she had—but as though every incident, beginning with this earliest, an approaching carriage, must be
noted, if only to be dismissed. Her disappointments having

all been reached, she gazed with eyes deadly impartial at the glaring white cubes of houses, and beyond them, at the sun-streaked stone wharf, the sea.

When she looked again to the carriage, she did so out of annoyance, for it entered town with an ancient, military clatter, as if cannon were its charge, battle its destination. Its driver, his Italian picture-postcard face bright with sweat, stood cracking his whip like a charioteer. At him Mrs. Markham did not look again, except to note that when the carriage halted before the locked and barred *pensione,* he came to his senses and sat down. Her attention was taken by, rather than given to, the passenger who, with his head thrown back, was staring up at her.

Impatience with his attitude was crushed in her when she felt he was looking at her more closely than it was usual for him to look at people. Also, it was not easy to look away from his eyes. They were brown eyes, muscular and privileged; and it was a lazy, sensual look they fixed on Mrs. Markham.

Emotionally visored, her own eyes betrayed none of the amazed uneasiness she felt when the passenger, luxuriating in a naïvete that one felt was hardly his, asked up to her, "It's too early, isn't it?"

Uncomplimented by this attention, Mrs. Markham decided it was due to fatigue and not to any real interest in

herself. Leaning over the balcony, she called down to him
to ring the bell.

"The bell . . . ?"

"It's there on the door, but rather high up," said Mrs.
Markham, and she looked away.

The bell was rung—she supposed by the driver—and the
doors of the *pensione* shot open. The carriage rolled away
with an air Mrs. Markham thought disconsolate. For the
driver sat with sloped shoulders, his whip limp in its holder,
and the horse's head hung fairly to its knees. What Mrs.
Markham felt about the stranger they had left behind was
that from her first uneasy sight of him she had begun
wanting to forget that she had seen him.

Now a bus passed, filled with schoolboys. Boys were
down over the wharf searching for things in the surf as
they did every morning. The old man was led from his
house across the street, his body peevish as a baby's being
diapered. Let go in the street, he shuffled free of the girl
who had led him, and inched his way into town alone.
Where in America, Mrs. Markham wondered, was there
time to wait so kindly, so dispassionately for someone to die?
The old man had had his time to live, and he was having
his time now to die. A little feast, a little procession, and
his time would be over. The girl would marry, have children, grow old, die. It would be ordinary.

Smiling to herself, Mrs. Markham wondered, Where in America—? But she had not time to go on, for a child-servant entered with her morning tea. She talked rapidly as she crossed the room:

"Signora Markham, the young man who has just arrived asked me who you were. 'Who is the lady on the balcony?' he said."

The child put the tea down, then put her hand to her sloppy mouth. "I told him. Was that right for me to do?"

Mrs. Markham came into the room with the faintest shade of threat in her step.

"Oh, I am so stupid," the child cried. "Yet I would not for the world, dear Signora Markham, do anything to displease you."

"You have not displeased me," Mrs. Markham told her.

"I am happy then, because I have not displeased either of you."

Mrs. Markham turned to the less disturbing view offered by her balcony. She lifted her tea to her mouth, hesitated before drinking, and searched the tray for sugar. There was none. "Miss Twilight," she said, but the child had slipped away.

Mrs. Markham, seized by a series of short, painful coughs, put down the teacup and went out again on the balcony. She regained her breath in the air, but not her composure; for two women dressed in black stopped their sewing to look up at her through their kitchen doorway. Their eyes, taking the glint of the steel needles, went through her and made her feel very silly indeed to have allowed a child to upset her.

Mrs. Markham had once been a schoolteacher, but so long ago that it was a wonder how she could sometimes look it. She looked it now, as, with an important little air, an air born of her feelings of impotence, she entered the dining room. Lowering her head, she walked with smaller steps than were usual to her and sat down longing for a menu to shield her. Of that resource she had no need, however, for the child, carrying a steaming silver bowl of soup, stood before her almost immediately. Her eyes, menacingly emotional, recorded with genuine pleasure Mrs. Markham's swift glance around the room at the empty tables.

"He is not here, Signora. He has friends—and letters. So many letters arriving here for him from Rome that we knew his name as well as if he'd been here all along. Didn't I tell you?"

No, Mrs. Markham had not been told. "Nor have you told me there would be no water with my meals," she said, indicating the empty pitcher on the table.

The child's eyes were ugly with tears when she returned

with the water. "I have displeased you," she said. "You will if you drop the pitcher," said Mrs. Markham, for it was a long time since one so young had oppressed her with his passion. Misfortune makes us sad and selfish, and Mrs. Markham was both. Recently, however, a resurgence of natural feeling had trickled from her to this little girl, a gray-faced waif from Naples, whose parents had got lost in the war; and Mrs. Markham, ignoring her real name of Antonia, had named her Miss Twilight.

Glowing with the pleasure of recognition, Antonia dared to ask, "Why?" "Because," replied Mrs. Markham, "you come knocking at this time of day." She had pointed to the darkening glass doors marked skimmingly with the flights of evening birds and bats. ". . . Twilight," she said, and she was lost in it. She had hardly felt Antonia's hot hand in hers as she watched, over the houses, boats being pulled up over the beach, where they sat through the night like beheaded swans.

Antonia had taken that offer of friendship to be as real as her own fingers, and as necessary. There had been no conflict calling for the show of allegiance, so Mrs. Markham was not, till this day, aware of what she had done. It had been left for the new arrival to uncover its full passion.

For born only this morning, but big enough in her now to kill her, was the little girl's desire that these two lovely

[8]

The Balcony

people, Signora Markham and Signor Sheridan, should be friends.

As Mrs. Markham rose from the table, she bent over and kissed the child. Whole worlds of sorrow begged up from Antonia's eyes, tears streamed down her face. Clutching Mrs. Markham about the thighs, she cried out with the remorse, not of a child but of an aged person, "I will never speak of him again, dear Signora Markham, never."

For the rest of the day Mrs. Markham avoided the *pensione*. Prolonging her afternoon walk, she stepped restlessly through the wild flowers growing on the edge of town, and wondered why it had even occurred to her to look back across the vineyards at the church clock. For the first time since her arrival, the spring, which she had followed down through Italy to this island, gave her, in place of a feeling of presentness, one of nostalgia. Poppies crimsoned the wild green grass at her feet. She wondered: Was it true that poppies were death's flower?

She took the path along the cliff, where she had dared only once before to walk, and tried not to see the smooth-backed rocks, the chunks of old gray lava in the water far away. But a pebble, disturbed by her foot, told her in an instant that she was very high indeed, and not the least indifferent to falling.

Friends and Vague Lovers

Smiling indulgently at her fear of disaster, for she took it gratefully as a sign of some humanness left her, Mrs. Markham left her precarious station for a safer, happier view.

Before her stretched a vineyard veiled in sunlight. The town shimmered beyond in the last heat of day. What buildings were white became yellow, and those that were yellow turned gold. Everything looked so arranged, so perfectly set and proportioned to the landscape, that it seemed not reality but art. So it remained till the sun went down. Then the golden light melted away. Raising her eyes to the sky, Mrs. Markham took dispirited note of some clouds which, like mythological horses, appeared to be waiting for night so they could descend and carry the island back to the mainland.

The sky had silvered by the time she arrived in town, and she could no longer see the clouds that had depressed her. Her eyes found pleasure in a shawl of roses over a molding arch, and in a cockeyed clothesline supporting the same red skirt, the same deflated shirt she had seen hanging there for weeks. Candles burned on shops' counters like votive lights. The electricity, if it did come on, and one was never sure, came on late. From the piazza rose a giant hum of voices which covered the town for quite a few yards like an umbrella of sound. There in the half-light men's faces gleamed like actors' wearing grease paint. Shirts gleamed more white, more pink than they truly were. And though there were not many, for it was a poor little town, those rings that were worn rode up and down the air on gesticulating fingers not like the cheap hand-me-downs they were, but preciously, finely, as if tradition had lent glitter where mere metal would have certainly failed.

The last town on the island, it seemed, at present, to be the last one on earth. All its lights were little, were nothing under the stars; but its men, occupied with the sea, the land, with heat and with cold, were as big perhaps as men could get to be. There was time here to remember. There *was* time, thought Mrs. Markham. No railroad had laid its ladder down here, nor were there signs that one would. The scene in the piazza moved back in time and consoled her. It was a yesterday she had heard about but had never seen. She experienced the pleasant sense of life having been lived before her, the sense that it would go on after her. Vesper bells pressed their message on the tail end of day. Men stepped aside for her. White shirts receded into the dark. Mrs. Markham felt the men had made a path for her, and they had, for she'd been standing in their midst.

She moved on down the street to the Pensione Morabido, where Antonia, having come so far, and with so many, stood as if frozen to the front steps. She had apparently infected the proprietor and his wife with her worry over Mrs. Markham's whereabouts, for they stood behind her smiling relieved smiles when their guest came up. They motioned her toward the dining room, which, lit garishly by a single flare of gas, showed Mrs. Markham the same steady pair of brown eyes that had studied her this morning, and were similarly studying her now.

Antonia waited conspiratorially for her employers to leave her in the hallway alone with Mrs. Markham. She had stepped to the side so that she could share with her friend a view of the dining room. When her employers retired to the back of the *pensione,* she stared sullenly and stubbornly up at Mrs. Markham as if they were both of them on the brink of something and there was now nothing to do but leap.

Suddenly she darted away. And then it was that she seemed truly twilight's child to Mrs. Markham. For she was near, yet quite out of one's reach, and not so much in the dark that she could not be seen, yet not enough out of it to be seen plainly. The reason for her running away came as a shock to Mrs. Markham when, turning away and preparing to mount the stairs, her eyes were caught and held by the flash of a napkin from the dining room. Stepping between her and the gaslight, the young man came darkly toward her.

She thought he smiled as he said, "Then you are Mrs. Markham, after all, aren't you?"

Mrs. Markham replied that she was.

"I'm a friend of Jonathan's," the dark face went on to say. "My name's Sheridan. Won't you come dine with me, and tell me all about him?"

"Jonathan . . . ?"

Sheridan hurried her hesitancy out of the way. "You are his mother, aren't you?"

"Jonathan's mother? Yes, I am, but . . ."

"I'm so sorry, Mrs. Markham, you must be tired. We can talk another time, can't we?" He moved away. "We'll meet again," he said.

"Yes," Mrs. Markham replied, "we'll meet again."

No sooner had he gone back to the dining room than Antonia rushed from her hiding place and flew halfway up the stairs to Mrs. Markham. "Don't," Mrs. Markham whispered, putting up her hand. "Now don't."

The child's outstretched arms did not go limp at this, but stiffened and widened as if to take in her friend's marvelous new dimensions. Her tight little chest heaved with greater and greater intensity of feeling as she piled make-believe image on image and saw Mrs. Markham, not as she was but as she wished her to be. Turning from the censorious hand, she leaped backwards and spun round and round at the foot of the stairs like one of the little dancing niggers in *Aida.*

In doing all this Antonia had made but the barest sounds. Her word not to mention Sheridan remained unbroken: What web she would spin would be spun in silence, thought Mrs. Markham, and she went to her room. She listened with relief when a round of applause from the dining room signified the end of the child's performance. It relieved her, not because it was applause but because it was the kind of applause it was. It was innocent, careless, and immediate. There was masculine density behind it; almost a goofiness. It was marvelously indifferent as to consequence. Mrs. Markham envied and despised its obtuseness. She herself would have liked to have been able to applaud the child in that manner, but because she knew she could not, she felt justified in giving the sensibilities of the applauder a very low grade indeed. Regretfully was this done; for during the half-lighted interview below, she had placed Sheridan quite high. She did not like being shown so soon that she'd been so wrong. Had he truly not seen something that, though it need not shock him, should have caused him to consider its possible effect on others? No, his had been nothing but the applause of dismissal, she decided, putting him back up again where she wanted him. Then she changed her clothes and went out on her balcony.

The Balcony

Down on the wharf, with his back to her, stood Sheridan. Indifference that had dripped from Mrs. Markham's eyes since this morning now drained from them. Her high place earlier on the cliff overlooking the sea seemed a footstool compared to how high she felt herself to be now. And her fall? How great that could be, she thought, as, bravely, she prepared to call Sheridan to her.

Of that she had no need. Sheridan, making no sound, turned to her.

The inevitableness of his doing so, of his standing carelessly below with his hands pocketed and unsurprised, made the surrounding night burn to mystic brightness for Mrs. Markham. This had happened so little to her, and when it had happened, so long ago that she felt every minute between the two experiences had been a long night of denial.

As Sheridan came to her, she did with him what her Miss Twilight was doing with her. She saw him as she wanted him to be, saying what she wanted him to say. She saw him as a vessel of thin glass ready to take what she would pour into it. It did not occur to her, as it might have earlier, that the vessel, contacting heat, might crack.

"Where is Jonathan, then, Mrs. Markham?" he asked precisely.

Mrs. Markham bent over the balcony. She was wearing an almost sheer pink dressing gown, which made her body look slight and physically anonymous. Her long, lean, dedicated face—the face of a solitary, passionate in the want of a craft, could have told her, had she been able to see it, that she was dreaming a dream. But it was the body anonymous she followed: billowing, skittish, pink.

"It seemed strange and impossible," she said, "to say it down there in the hall, and it seems stranger still to say it from here, Mr. Sheridan. But we can't go on this way, can we? You thinking and acting as if Jonathan could be here. You see, Mr. Sheridan, Jonathan's dead."

The face below her changed with breathless swiftness. It grew younger, as indeed it should have done, for it was the face, suddenly, of a child whose curiosity has brought it to the unexpected. It did not know where it was, nor did it know what to do. It had been jolted out of time, pushed beyond its power to comprehend, and it could do nothing but look forward to sneaking away. All urgency departed from the young man below.

"Then there is nothing to say, is there?" he said, taking even that right from her.

Mrs. Markham agreed that, no, there was not.

She smiled at the animal bite he had taken out of a moment that she had prepared to be so grand. She dared not look down again; for, she wondered, hadn't he swaggered away?

The Balcony

What made her forgive him, rather—she did not know then it was to be perhaps his sole attraction for her—was Sheridan's insistence, silently given, but given out through every pore of his body, that he had nothing to do with death. This was straightforward and honest. It shone in his healthy hair, his handsome face. I am alive, it said, and I only understand being alive. What he had actually said was mean and evasive. He was a person whose legs were quicker than his mind, so all he could do was to revert without glory to his childhood when no one had bothered to tell him such a thing. He had asked of the quick and had been told of the dead, and he felt the bewilderment of deception.

Mrs. Markham's sense of irony, though developed, went soft as smoke against what Sheridan had left with her. So numerous were the images that filled her eyes when she first closed them that it was not till she had dragged a chair out to her balcony and sat upright and terrified to wait for morning that she was able to close them again.

[*Chapter Two*]

Mrs. markham had not thought much of any man till she had given birth to one. Mr. Markham, who had married her out of innocence, never was so alive to her as the day she left him. Before she had reason to do that, Markham had taken her from schoolteaching in Middle-Western America down across the Andes to Peru. For like many of his kind his interest was in places, not persons. Indians black-shawled, churches half earthquaked away, were place to him. Lima perpetually clouded, taking honey-eyed revenge on its old conqueror's skeleton perpetually displayed, was a dream come true to Markham, who had so exhausted himself as a boy with the future that he was more than grateful to the present when he reached it.

He was an engineer, and a very good one; but Alice Markham, when she thought of him at all, saw him vaguely as a little man who liked to undress in front of her. He was a little man, it was true, far bigger within than he was without, but of this Mrs. Markham was unaware. His only lie, and a dangerous one had he persisted in it, was to pretend at first to share his passion for place with Alice. He soon admitted to himself what he had known all along, that pleasure is private and can be shared only with one who seeks it with you. So keeping his wisely to himself, Markham let Mrs. Markham wait for hers to come along.

Bound by contract and by nothing else, they moved across South America like business associates with no business to do with each other. Jonathan, when he did come, was business enough, but so completely was he snapped up by Mrs. Markham, that Markham, wondering exquisitely if he had had anything to do with the child before its birth, knew he'd never again come so near it as he had when creating it. Ah—but there was Lima, and Bogota, and Valparaiso; he smelled the sticky sweet air of Barbados, and thought of his favorite, Lima, again.

The Balcony

Born to travel, he cared not to establish vague replicas of home. For with his poignant sense of privacy and place, he carried about with him all the home he desired. His roots were above ground, Markham's, and they stretched from country to country, and were thin and airy as lace.

Mrs. Markham decided on Jonathan the minute she felt him, and the minute she felt him, she felt herself. For she had been steered by Markham to discover a land, and she had seen two gulls come out of the night; she had seen a leaf on the water, and she had dreamed while Markham had slept, of a green land which must be hers—all of it— though she had to kill Markham to get all of it. She had not to kill anybody, of course, for they were both alike in their profound inability to share each other's pleasures. Markham, recognizing hers had come along at last, let her go.

So away she went with her little money, which was not so little, and with Jonathan, who was as big a thing as Alice Markham had ever known.

It was natural she should come to New England, which is, after all, not a place but a way of life. There, the doors of her mind long closed to the exotic, now opened to it. There, in a town east of Boston, Mrs. Markham dipped back into her travels and carried Jonathan about in a sack on her back as she had seen the Peruvian Indians do with their prune-eyed offspring. But she was a secret eccentric, happily without the need to display her extravagances beyond the walls of her house, where, though they would have escaped reprimand, they would certainly not have gone unnoticed.

A piercing sense of insecurity lifted a peal of laughter from Mrs. Markham when Jonathan, having just turned ten, gave indications that she bored him. She felt naked. For the first time in her life Alice Markham wanted to be other than what she was: she would be perfect or she would be nothing. She preferred being a thing next to him, necessary to him as his coat, rather than a mother who failed to amuse him.

Sharpened, rather than numbed, by her sense of possible loss, Mrs. Markham shrewdly stepped aside and let Jonathan open all the small doors he wanted to open rather than close the biggest one on her. What he saw outside, and what he learned, grew in him to the extent that in less than a year Mrs. Markham stood silent, conniving behind him while he gazed at a Velasquez infanta and knew about the Prado before he was quite sure of Spain.

He was a dark, attentive boy whose attention, when forced elsewhere than he chose to direct it, brought from him a perhaps too willing masochism. He sat for long hours suffering through movies with her before Mrs. Markham discovered he did not like them, or preferred attending them alone. His revolts, though silent and incomplete, never quite stopped coming, and were never expected by her when they did come. She feared them not nearly so much as she feared the time when Jonathan would know what they were and how they affected her.

Her life, from this time on, consisted of a series of anticipatory efforts on her part to give Jonathan an interest in which she had a share before he found one himself and cut her out. Anxious lest he shoot away on summer excursions with friends his own age, she moved him every spring out to Cape Cod, that shaggy finger of land, crooked as though calling the rest of the world to it—Mr. Markham would have said, archly: lucky for the world it had not heard. There, Jonathan's interest mounted through the summers like a kite with him alone holding the string they had once held together. Assisted and directed by tutors Mrs. Markham avoided meeting, his talent grew equally with his talent for keeping it to himself.

He was inside the egg of his interest and she was outside waiting for the crack she saw in it to widen. For his interest, she felt, was not in himself, but in others; his passion for their achievements drew strength from his own endeavors, and would leave him muscleless and unfit for competition when that time arrived. Mrs. Markham desired the crack to widen to let her in, but not the truth, which would, she feared, break the egg and perhaps break Jonathan.

Actually her treachery frightened her. She indulged it so far as to wait, but some vague horror of consequence held her back from telling him what she knew he would one day find out for himself. And that perhaps is why she thought of Europe.

There the egg grew very crowded indeed. What pathos Mrs. Markham might have enjoyed at the sight of Jonathan's enthusiasms in the long galleries was shelved in her for a later day when she could not enter one without seeing again the black-haired boy who quite frequently had not seen her: "My goodness, Jonathan, don't you recognize me? I'm your mother." "Oh Mother, of course I do—now." He would smile, take her hand, look away again. A guard directed him up from a bench in the Vatican where he had been lying so as to see better the swirling painted figures on the ceiling above. "You're as bad as a foreigner," Mrs. Markham complained afterwards, laughing. For she had not recognized the young man the chapel guard was tapping, tapping on the soles of his feet, till the young man had risen. "Why Jonathan Markham! Lying there like...! Well, goodness!"

The Balcony

One hot, sun-brown day in Spain, Mrs. Markham sat alone in one of those cool courts in the Alhambra, soothed by the playing fountain and the fact that Jonathan was close by though she could not see him. Rheita-like music winding upward from somewhere in the town below turned her body to it dancing, though she had not danced before, and though she did not rise, hardly moved. Her eyes, coaxed upward by columns breathlessly twisting, gazed into the hot blue square of sky above, then down at a tiny window through which Jonathan looked at her but, seeing her so absorbed, silently withdrew.

Later, in the evening of that same day, Mrs. Markham and Jonathan paused in their dinner to watch the antics of a waiter chasing an owl that had somehow got into the dining room of their hotel. When the waiter had caught the owl, he seemed disappointed he had done so so quickly and so soon. He was not disappointed in himself, naturally, but in the owl.

Adored during the chase, the owl was despised now in captivity. Squashing it in a nasty feather bundle between his hands, the waiter peevishly crossed the terrace and tossed the owl, with an oath, over the balustrade.

Falling no more than a few yards down, the owl, which had appeared so small, stopped, or appeared to stop, there in the air, and spreading great wings, flew triumphantly out over the lights which were then coming on in Granada.

Friends and Vague Lovers

Jonathan pressed both arms on the balustrade and watched long after it.

"Father would like it," he said at last.

"Father?"

Deep emotion impoverishes the face: anger, regret dash over it like pale soldiers both fighting on the wrong side; hope sits in back of the eyes horrified at its own existence. Mrs. Markham trembled as she asked, "Were you speaking to me, Jonathan, or to . . . ?"

"To Granada," he replied.

Longing for the Peruvian sack she had carried Jonathan in as a baby, Mrs. Markham was pleased, rather than not, by the pitchforks pointing into the bright sky over Barcelona, the truckloads of Red-saluting men and women on their way to Madrid, the burning houses, churches, and fields everywhere, when Spain, caught in its civil war, told her what she already knew: that she'd better get Jonathan and herself home.

Grateful to this event, she would not be grateful to any others. For inevitable as it was, the war when it reached her in New England in 1941, shocked her; but when it took Jonathan, who was then twenty-five, it outraged her.

"But Jonathan, your career," she cried.

This particular cloak of belief did not fit her and Jonathan knew it. So leaving her with a little pity, he went off to what might have been war had he been lucky; but Jonathan was not lucky, so he spent three boring, wasted years minding weather stations, mostly in the South.

What Mrs. Markham always wanted for Jonathan was that nothing should happen to him. This wish appeared to have been granted her again when, on his return from the army, he gave no hint that anything had happened. She knew he would return intact, she desired that he should, and he did. It was inevitable with a kind of inevitableness that Mrs. Markham appreciated.

Deep in her lay a cold, hard belief that had never been more cold, more hard. It was that Jonathan had no friend but Alice Markham, no real interest but her. Preciously she guarded this belief, wisely she had never brought it to light. For, indeed, it might have melted under any but the crude little light she had chosen to cast on it.

She considered Jonathan went away too often now; received too many letters. She said nothing. For when he was with her he was all with her, and she was content, though watchful. Gradually, too, his interest that had once frightened her, that interest she had seen as an egg meant to crack, showed signs of having done so. Jonathan's youthful talent had flared truly and widely enough for a boy, it was true; but to a man with a man's knowledge of what other men have done and are doing it was only a candle doomed to go out.

Mrs. Markham might have asked for no more than that this candle should burn between them again, that Jonathan should sit drawing, over and over again, her hands, eyes, her long, narrow head, as he had done before the war. But she was not, if truth be known, ever happy with Jonathan except when she had carried him next to her, a helpless, lazy-eyed baby in a Peruvian sack who moved when she moved, and not before.

One evening as they sat together, Mrs. Markham lifted her hand and examined her nails with downcast eyes.

"Jonathan," she said, "you must do something now, something for yourself—in *earnest*, Jonathan."

Jonathan raised eyes confessing defeat.

Tacking wings to her heart, he replied in a fumbling, embarrassed voice that, yes, she was right, he must—do something.

Those wings, alas, were not meant to fly; for Mrs. Markham had forgotten her old prophecy, and it is as bad to forget a prophecy made as it is to make one and never forget it. Egg indeed! Are we to recall our littlest fantasy at such shining times? Jonathan had grown up. He would soon need glasses, she suspected: a pity, for his eyes were rather like Markham's—startlingly blue eyes, too, Markham's, for so indifferent a man.

The Balcony

So she continued up to the morning of Jonathan's departure for—Rhode Island? she thought, but she was not certain. It was a winter morning. Jonathan's bag stood packed in the front hall, Mrs. Markham noted, as she came down to bid him good-by.

"Jonathan," she said, "you mustn't take things so seriously." Placing penitent hands on his coat, she said, "Of course you have your career." But career was a word she had used with such noticeable infrequency in the past that it refused to budge now in emergency. Jonathan replied with a look so cynical that she flew to the door and opened it for him. She wanted him out of the house; suddenly she wanted him amongst the friends she had denied his ever having. "You'll miss your train. Hurry!"

"Oh no. I've given myself plenty of time."

"Yes, you're like your father in that," she said, for she needed everything.

Laughing tolerantly at the ease with which she reached back to a past she had on all other occasions wanted dead, Jonathan told her to close the front door: he said he'd forgotten something in the studio.

The studio, a small one-room building heated by a coal stove Jonathan himself stoked and kept going during the winter days and nights he worked there, was only a few yards from the main house. It took him time to open the door, for it was locked; and he had to search his key ring for the key. After he had closed the door behind him, Mrs. Markham's panic broke over her in a wave. She reached the studio just as the bullet shot that killed Jonathan went off. Her hands, which had already taken hold of the doorknob, continued to turn it slowly and heavily, as though a vital part of her was turning with it. She fell through the open door to the floor. Folding her hands in exasperation, she rose and did not unfold them until she had kicked the door closed and picked up the revolver. She raised it to the clear space between her eyes. Pressing the trigger, she fell to her knees asking the air every inch of the way down why Jonathan had not left a bullet for her.

Masqueraded in the coat Jonathan had last worn, she replied, later, to questions concerning Mr. Markham's whereabouts, that she presumed him to be dead. She was wrong. People like Markham go unharmed. Obeying nothing else, they obey the sign of the wanderer, the nomad, the sign of the adventurer who knows in his heart he is no adventurer. Their only worry is that their attachment to loneliness will be found out and taken from them. In Lima this is not likely to happen. There, where violence seldom visits one man at a time, rarities like Markham are let be.

[*Chapter Three*]

THE MORNING FOLLOWING her aborted interview with
Sheridan, Mrs. Markham was awakened by Good Friday
cannon fire. Stumbling up from the chair on her balcony
where she had spent the night, she dragged closed the
shutters, brought in her chair, and went to bed. There,
while the day built pale ladders of light out of her shutters, and while the cannon in the hills throbbed giant answers to the church bells in the town, Mrs. Markham
dreamed of time past and time present, and of a timeless
time blended of both.

Friends and Vague Lovers

Across the field of her dream, which was strewn with the odds and ends of war, rode Sheridan dressed in the costume of an ancient Greek. He was beating his horse forward through carnage. Rearing upward, the horse sent stars flying from its mane which, on striking earth, went out. Thus the horse manifested its revolt against Sheridan, whom it loved beyond all things, for dragging the body of Jonathan between the rows of the fallen over weeds and broken swords.

"Why have you turned traitor to me?" Sheridan cried.

"Because you have turned traitor to yourself," replied the horse in a human voice; but keeping his remaining stars, precious as life to them both, he reared upward no more.

Swords stuck out of the earth as numerously as do the reproachful needles of the cactus plunge at the harmless air, but Mrs. Markham felt no remorse about what they had done to Jonathan, for his wounds closed as she looked at them. Close curls fitted his head like a cap, his eyes were blind-blue as a sailor's eyes, and his mouth, like the mouths of distant soldiers, was dressed in a final, mocking smile.

Surprised that she could see soldiers so far away, Mrs. Markham wondered, was it true what she felt, that all of them were fighting away from their native lands? Dying up the mountainside, they did so with their heads turned

from one another, and with a look of unfinished business in
their eyes.

Delicious approval of what Sheridan had done with
Jonathan rippled like laughter through Mrs. Markham's
blood, but she feared to show her treachery before the intelligent horse; for then he might cast off stars again, and it
was the stars, precious to them both, that Sheridan loved.

When more cannon went off, Mrs. Markham, who had
assumed the battle to be over, watched without dismay, but
carefully, the curtain of her dream cautiously part on the
picture of St. Vitus hanging on the wall of her bedroom
at the *pensione.*

A knock on her door shot her sufficiently far into the
present to cause her to reach guiltily for a book beside her
bed and to open it to hide the fact that she'd slept so late.
"Come in," she said in a voice whose theatrical honey
poured only so long as the door remained closed. When it
opened, and showed Mrs. Markham her caller, nothing
was left her but silence, confusion, and chagrin.

"Oh I'm so sorry, Mrs. Markham," he said, seeing her
still in bed.

He turned to go, then turned again and faced her with
an air of having as much right to be there as the daylight.

"I have barged in, Mrs. Markham," he said, "but that's
not half as bad as barging away, as I feel I did last night.

when I stopped you from talking. It's silly, I know, because nothing ever comes twice but trouble, does it? but I wish, I do wish you could tell me what you wanted to tell me, now."

Mrs. Markham's book slipped from her hands like silk. Her eyes were bright, but negative; her feelings sweetly sick at having at her disposal the power to refuse him, which she did in a voice wincing beneath the stings of self-inflicted pain.

"Now, Mr. Sheridan?" she asked, begging him not to believe her. "Now, in this bright light?"

But he did believe her. He had come halfway in, and now, with her help, he would go the whole way out. Only a diamond-hard part of Mrs. Markham had refused him, he knew. Otherwise, why should she have listened to him as though every word he had said was food to her. "No, it would not be possible, would it, in this light?" he replied, and slipped out the door.

The second he was out of sight Mrs. Markham felt she had never before seen anyone go that she wanted so badly to stay. Taking her book into her hands, she opened it and tore out page after page, saying in bitter mimicry of herself, "In this bright light, Mr. Sheridan? In this bright light?"

Her reason had told her to say that, so she maligned it. And as she did, she felt it give way, grow soft and shape-

less as a cloud. Offering nothing but the ice-cold advice
that no move is better than a wrong one, her reason had
someday to melt, and now it had. It melted in her remorse
at having sent away Sheridan, and it melted in the red
pageant of her return to something like desire. Yet the
holes in her reason closed for long enough, and often
enough, to warn her she had once been vanquished. Was
she not satisfied with peace?

Dressing hurriedly, Mrs. Markham supposed that no,
she was not, and went down to lunch.

No sooner had her foot touched the stair landing in the
lower hall, than Miss Twilight, addressing the proprietor's
wife in an auditorium voice, said, "The new one left."

"Why do you tell me, Antonia?" the proprietor's wife
replied. "I already know. And don't shout like a soldier."

"But about his letters . . . ?"

"I know that also, idiot."

"Yes, but you told me to remind you."

"I told you nothing," the bedeviled woman cried, charg-
ing at her torturer, who slipped away from her out the
front door. "She is a good worker," the proprietor's wife
told Mrs. Markham, "but I worry no longer as to the contents of her head." Whirling a pointed finger at her own
temple, she closed one of her pretty eyes in a wink:
"Empty, Signora, empty."

Wishing this were so, Mrs. Markham opened the door

on the people in the procession, whose Good Friday sorrow failed to match her own. For whereas hers was new and pruned to privacy, their's was older than anything they wore, and theatrical and natural as a storm. Celebrating a great sorrow relieved them of their own, but of this Mrs. Markham was unaware, for it was precisely her own that she celebrated.

Out in the center of the crowd beneath the plaster Virgin, whose tears protruded from her face and were white, leaped Antonia, whose own face, turned to Mrs. Markham, conveyed more hope than it did sense. Anticipating Easter Sunday, ignorant of Gethsemane, and that there was yet to follow the further Agony on the Cross, the child was happy amongst hundreds of people who knew enough not to be otherwise than sad.

Ignoring the death without which there would not be half the joy in rebirth there is, Antonia raised a jubilant cry there in the middle of the knowing, somber, sunburnt crowd, and, clutching at the shirts of the men carrying the Virgin Mary, tossed a bunch, big as springtime, of wisteria onto the little platform at Mary's feet. For this she deserved and got a crack on the head, which she acknowledged no more than Mary had her flowers. Darting out of the procession, she whispered, "From me to the Virgin for you, dear Signora Markham."

The Balcony

This was too much for Mrs. Markham, who, leaving her, followed the procession for as long as it lasted.

The day wore a face sullen as museum armor. Pieces of sunlight fell on bawling donkeys, on narrow-backed, sickle-tailed dogs. Misery and the miserable dominated the procession. It was the hags one saw, the hawk-faced matrons, the silly ones with dyed hair, and not the strong-legged men with black hair curling where their shirts opened at the neck, or the blond ones with almond-pale eyes. Like any agony the procession appeared to be lasting forever till, moving out into the open at the edge of town, it stopped.

There, the Virgin's silver-starred mantle rose in the wind like a sob, and fell, and rose widely again as she rode into church. Small boys tugged bells in the church tower. Cannon blasted from the hills. Firecrackers sputtered along the sea wall. Bells, cannon, firecrackers rang, blasted, and sputtered, till the island, ringed in a sky-crashing band of sound, seemed to bulge, split with a cry to heaven for approval. Then all was silent as the black air above the crowd in the wide church doorway, and as the rain falling so wide apart as to be scarcely noticed.

Mrs. Markham stood with a cowl-faced boy, who, the minute she noticed him, dropped to his knees and gathered into his hands a few of the thousands of pebbles in front of the church. These he poured from hand to hand. He grew frantic when he dropped one, and lowered his face as he searched the ground for the pebble he had lost. For it was the precise one that was precious to him, and he would not know, as Mrs. Markham, watching him, did, that every time he dropped a pebble he replaced it with another.

Searching her handbag, she threw the deluded boy some lira, but when it reached the wet pebbles, shame made her kneel with the boy and help him retrieve it. Close to hers, his face sickened her. Premature wrinkles crisscrossed it like threads, and all the threads ran through his chapped skin to his ears, both of which twirled in pink-blue points at their tips. Doing nasty penance, Mrs. Markham knelt thus till the church swelled with prayer. Then she rose and hurried away as the organ made music as reluctant as the rain was to fall and moisten the parched air, the heads and shoulders of people, and their faces and the face of the world.

All her points of interest had fallen, withered, turned to plaster and ash in her eyes as surely as if they'd been bombed. At the sea she was struck in the face by a strong new sheet of rain. The wind rose to let the sky attain that pitch of darkness it had been aiming at all day.

On the path along the cliff Mrs. Markham's frustrations

subsided somewhat as she watched a rowboat poke about
in the water between the rocks below. The boatman stood
up rowing, and the passenger sat. It was the sight of the
passenger that startled her; he that made her lean forward
with stiffened arms and clutch her coat in her hands as
though it were bread she'd been starving for.

What no procession, no image, no replaying of a re-
ligious tragedy, no humanness destroyed by infirmity, no
trailing misery from one end of the town to the other had
been able to do for her, was done for her now by a man in
a boat.

"I've been led here," Mrs. Markham whispered believ-
ingly.

She stared. She bent forward. She desired both to be,
and not to be, recognized. Was it real? The very possibility that it was not fascinated her; for she was in the
dangerous position of not wanting to believe her eyes if her
eyes denied what she wanted them most to see. But she had
been right, he was here.

Devotedly she searched the details of the scene whose
center gave her once more, Mrs. Markham felt, something
to live for. Beginning with joyous thanksgiving, she went
through anger, touched malice with, What's he doing out
in a boat on a day like this? Serves him right if it does
capsize!, then settled down again to steady, devotional examination. Sheridan, innocent of the net of feeling she had

thrown down around him, stared upward in her direction; but whether to see her or not Mrs. Markham never knew.

His look was beatified, helpless. His hands clutched the sides of the boat, his feet were bare, and in his lap lay his shoes. Behind him, bent over his oars like a strongly opinionated midget who had decided nothing in the world was higher than himself, was the boatman. There was no other boat for as far as the eye could see on the angry green water.

When the boatman rowed out from between the rocks and pointed his prow toward town, Mrs. Markham followed it, but not for long. Her path turned inland, while their's turned out around the island to the other side of the sea wall. Out of sight, it was not out of mind. Lacking sails itself, it gave Mrs. Markham so many that in less than half the time it usually took her, she found herself back at the *pensione* and out on her balcony with but the faintest recollection of having come through town at all. Still wearing her wet coat, which was Jonathan's and which she still wore, she watched the sea wall, the beach, the wharf.

The sky, which had churned with murderous gray quiet most of the day, let drop its sullen mask and showed now a face of red gold. Snow-white clouds tumbled their buttocks to the sun; and the sea winked up at them like a gay old sport with a million eyes for pleasure. But Mrs. Markham, pinched by her sense of time needed, stared at the red sun as if by doing so she could hold it still. Nothing was still, nothing waited as she waited. Time turned traitor to her, took the island to night; and the island, judging from the townspeople chatting on the wharf below, was heartlessly eager to go.

Hopeless herself, Mrs. Markham longed to see hopelessness on every stone. The sun went down and stars showed bright over the darkening sea. Trees closed their eyes, and evening birds opened theirs. White shirts gleamed against the wharf's black stones, but Sheridan's was not amongst them.

Turning to her room—for the outside world had betrayed her—Mrs. Markham begged everything she looked at to come to life and help her. She believed in magic now that she needed it, and would have fallen on her knees to a stick had one bent to help her.

Many times she imagined Sheridan walking through the throng on the wharf, but imagining so did not really place him there, nor did it help. When the light went on out on the sea wall, Mrs. Markham closed her eyes.

Thus she gave, in her misery, meaning to the most meaningless things, and would have paid primitive homage to a dog had she heard one howl.

No, he would not come. The sea was black and had taken him, and he could not come.

Leaving her with a piece of joy she had only tried on,

but with enough pain to wear forever, Sheridan had drowned. Turn where she would in a hope for pleasure Mrs. Markham felt her journey was all downward going. Why, she pondered, had she to learn it again? Closing the windows to her balcony, she replied to Antonia in the doorway that she would be down in a moment to dinner.

In the dining room, Mrs. Markham warded off with a holy smile some picnic greetings thrown her by two sets of fat Swiss just arrived. There was spaghetti *al burro,* which she ate with good appetite. She did not look up till the fish came, and she would not have done so then had not the fish—awful little red monsters with their heads on—needed more attention than she felt up to giving them. Turning as far from the Swiss as she could, and looking as little as was necessary at Antonia, Mrs. Markham stared straight at Sheridan, who for a man she'd imagined drowned, was very dry indeed. He had eaten well—as well, one felt, as he always did, for he smiled at the Swiss, but not at her, and got up swiftly and left.

It was not until Mrs. Markham was well into the center of town after him that she realized how ridiculously she was behaving. Giving only the barest heed to this aspect of her conduct, she rushed on till she was near enough to Sheridan to talk to him, and also to see that she could not. The shock of seeing so much of him here beneath one of the two lights hanging low over the piazza made Mrs. Markham realize how impossible it would have been for Sheridan to drown. She burned with shame as she remembered she had spent the afternoon thinking he could.

Stepping into the dark beneath some trees siding the piazza, Sheridan entered what Mrs. Markham thought of as a large dirty square of amber-colored light. Other times, and in the same light, she would have admitted it was a café. A bamboo-beaded curtain showering down the doorway jerked the café from side to side like a kite, striped and crowded. Sparkles of heatfat whirled around electric bulbs and bathed the backs of card players in oily light. Light wine and red gleamed on the bar beside a coffee machine which was dull and cozy as the eyes of the proprietresses. They watched the café's occupants with faces of women who have heard the same joke often. The tallest and eldest had a face self-centered as an owl's. Her sisters had plain women's faces, and fat, sleepy breasts, which they leaned on all night long. Love for their customers sat secure behind the boredom in all their eyes.

Sun-stain rather than sunburn was not all that gave Sheridan a look theatrical; for he moved, and perhaps lived, with the curtain always raised, as it were, on himself; and, though he would move over for someone else, there was, in essence, always only himself. He was the-

atrical in that he pointed up his surroundings to the extent
of making you wonder what he was doing in them, how
he got to them, and when he would leave. Lacings of pink
match sticks, and cigarette butts, lay in a dry little sea of
ash at his feet, which were, Mrs. Markham remarked, a
trifle dapper. His air of keeping his troubles to himself was
too pointedly gracious not to be disquieting.

Refusing a chair offered him by his friends, he stood
as though he were tacitly acknowledging their right and
his to escape boredom by whatever means possible. But
his friends, ignorant of the fact that they were not obliged
to imprison one another in a wall of boredom thicker than
stone, sat with that drugged look achieved by people who
frequent the same café night after night with the same
people. These Mrs. Markham checked off like a column of
figures whose sum total was small as she desired it should
be. They were Americans, rather elderly young men, some,
whose attire reached a few too many summers back to suit
them now.

When Sheridan came toward her, Mrs. Markham did
not realize he meant to come all the way. For he bent suddenly to his friends and talked to them for the first time.
However, he was as quick to descend on people, apparently, as he was to leave them, and his hand was through
the bead curtain before she could move away.

The Balcony

"Ah, Mrs. Markham," he said, frowning. "How nice to see you, Mrs. Markham."

"I'm afraid I'm in the wrong place,". Mrs. Markham said, hardly concealing the fact that if so she was glad of it.

"I wouldn't say that," Sheridan replied, meaning that he couldn't.

They stood for seconds staring at each other like strangers who have suddenly found out more about each other than they know what to do with. Then Sheridan took her by the arm, and in doing so touched her coat with the rather unpleasant sensation of having touched it before. Like wearing somebody's skin, he thought, and rather than take her so soon into the dark he held her there in the light of the doorway.

Pointing into the café, he said, "So you've been watching the Macaroni, Mrs. Markham, haven't you?"

"The Macaroni?"

"Yes, you know, all of us traveling and aping; traveling and aging. All of us being more and more as we were when we left home!—No, that's not true; but it's so perfect, isn't it, the Macaroni? And so right you should see us, Mrs. Markham, through these." He ran his hand over the curtain, which ticked like castanets heard from far off.

No. Jonathan's shadow slipped away illusive as a penny

in the hands of a magician when Mrs. Markham attempted picturing him around the café table, his feet in the pink match sticks, the cigarette ash. No.

"You know, Mr. Sheridan," she said, "I don't believe you knew Jonathan well?"

Showing far less impatience with her than he felt, Sheridan released her arm and went off alone into the dark beneath the trees. Mrs. Markham went to him with her hand to her mouth.

"No, Mrs. Markham," he said, "I did not know Jonathan well. Is that a crime? Will it be a crime if I say, later, that I didn't know you terribly well, or if you say it of me?"

"A crime, Mr. Sheridan?" Reaching far more back into her own experience than she would dare admit, Mrs. Markham replied in a voice peculiar to people who say what they please about life, if only because they are about to leave it, that not to know certain people well, could be a crime.

"But we're not speaking of certain people," said Sheridan.

"We're not?"

"Jonathan was a friend, but not a close friend, or at least not close for very long."

"For as long as you would let him."

The Balcony

"I doubt if you have the right to accuse me of Jonathan, Mrs. Markham."

"I did, didn't I?" she cried, taken aback rather, for she had not thought him so bright.

Smiling, she moved out from the dark into the lighted piazza.

There, what might have been said beneath the trees, or before the half-lit café to the ticking of bamboo beads, could not now be said. Here in the piazza not a paper moved, not a light burned but those two above. Every stone told a story without words. It was such a time as lovers know, and people who hate each other intimately know well. A dragging time, an inching time, a time when a fear of consequence makes breathing the wildest folly. So it was odd that these two, having but recently met, should feel it.

Everything said seemed now to have been nothing said: small talk outside a small café, no more. Now every step they took threatened to prologue a saga. Sheridan, hoping his silence would pass as shyness, tried to understand what caused Mrs. Markham's. For that he had not long to wait.

They had to be let into the *pensione,* and it was then, after Sheridan had rung the bell, that Mrs. Markham turned to him. For she needed the pressure of time to give her as little time as possible to say what she might not have been able to say otherwise, and perhaps might never have said had she not dreamed so treacherously that morning.

As the door opened, she gave one long "Who are you?" look at the poor proprietor, and passing him without a word, addressed herself to Sheridan as they mounted the stairs:

"I have the feeling that you fear a story from me. Please don't, because I have none to tell. I would prefer to see this as the beginning of a friendship, and not the continuation of one, don't you agree?"

Sheridan replied that he did.

"After all," she said, pinning him to it, "it wasn't I who knew you before, was it? Good night, Sheridan."

Downstairs the proprietor slammed the shutters close, and closed and locked the door. Sheridan hurried down to catch him before he got back into bed. For the door was devilishly hard to open, as he had previously found out. The proprietor, looking comically like a man nobody liked, gave Sheridan a key to let himself back in with.

Exulting in the fact that there is an outside to even the worse things, Sheridan tore up the street from the *pensione*. Unfortunately Mrs. Markham was on her balcony, but he pretended she was not.

Inside the café, which was now candle-dim and empty,

The Balcony

Sheridan dropped the key the proprietor had given him.
Picking it up, he thought of Jonathan: "Throw down my
key, my key," the Irishman shouted. And so they did.
Poor Mikey. Poor Jonathan. It was very funny.

The three sisters sat out from the bar on chairs. Patches
of blue smoke lazed around their faces, for they were all
three enjoying a cigarette. There was no one else there.
"Look you two," said the eldest one to her sisters in a voice
whose compassion rung low and stayed long, like the
sound of a night guitar, "attend to Signor Sherry, for he
is alone and wanting."

PART II: *The Macaroni*

[*Chapter Four*]

SHERIDAN'S GREAT GIFT was that when people saw him they knew what they wanted. This made him as much hated as he was loved, and frequently by the same kind of person. Those who were quite different, and despised him, Sheridan dismissed as being not real. Thus was it remarked that his childhood must have been unhappy; for he talked of it as though it existed only where he wanted it to, which more often than not was in no place at all.

That he let it be known he came from a county no one

ever heard of, or a town in Florida new as false teeth, was bad enough; but when the town was shifted North, and the county pushed all the way down to include San Antonio, Texas, where he had been stationed for awhile during the war, those who loved Sheridan threw up their hands in surrender to the impression he gave them they liked most, that of having just appeared.

His coats were never buttoned, nor were his eyes ever quite closed. He never walked slowly if he could walk fast, and he seldom walked if he could ride. He seemed always to be verging a corner, and more likely than not he was. Not a great deal of him had to pretend to be unable to sleep when he thought someone he knew might be awake nearby; but he could sleep successfully in trains, buses, cars, and churches, and had once slept straight through till sundown on a bench in the Tuileries following an unhappy lunch with a friend who had shown up so changed and fat and red in the face that Sheridan, too depressed to eat, had gotten drunk enough to depart under the guise of not knowing what he was doing.

Pretending undue love of nature, he went silent as a cat on a beach, turned pale with boredom in the country, and sought in the latter an arrangement of the scene rather than the scene itself, which was always too big for him.

What he did was to put pieces of country back in the

city, where he felt in his heart they belonged. Parisian squares, like the one called Furstenburg, he adored. For though it was the fearful city he loved, it was nature that could put him to his knees. Naturally he was up and away like a shot the first chance he got; and it was his chances, which Sheridan lived openly by, that gave him his grievance against the future simply because it was the future and not the past.

Despite his moving about, his air of freedom and well-being, he was singularly lacking in will. What seemed most natural to him was a state of being adored. About this he was often necessarily impatient, but never selfish. He had been moved for so long and so often by people who had taken him up that he now failed to realize his flight to this island was not due to himself but, as always, to someone else. Certainly it was not what he was beginning to think it was, a sentence passed on himself by himself alone.

It being in his nature to attract people who were as demanding as he was not, Sheridan's protection against them was impatience. Impatience he had, and impatient he was when he left Rome. The thought that his flight could be turned into exile had not yet completely occurred to him. Otherwise he would have listened more closely to the unease he felt, standing now smiling at the three sisters in the sad café.

Friends and Vague Lovers

Aware though he was that pleasure can be anything but continuous, Sheridan sought continuity nowhere else. One frequently pictured him as a child waiting through three rainy days for the sun to come light up the street; and when it did, Sheridan running to get it every bit, but not once forgetting how he had waited through those days of rain. The essence of his nature was longing.

What made him superior to persons who were similarly apprehensive as to the future and silent about their past was that Sheridan would not say he was. In this lay his pride, deep as it was hidden. In this Mrs. Markham had dreamed true: he would not have buried his own mother, let alone Jonathan, for he had not that brand of courage. His courage was of a sentimental variety; his battle dress as changeable and light as light; but his lance had been darted as hard, as sure, and as often as the lances of far hardier men—men who have no sooner thrown their's than another is given them by tradition, by friends, and by their families. Sheridan had no one standing by.

He had been taken up for amusement and knew well the sensation of being let down. Left horseless on a field of not much honor, he had to forget the past and get what he could the moment he could.

If men were judged for how far they've come from home, then Sheridan's score would have stood high as a sailor's, were it not that a sailor—and indeed all men—must return home to prove that he's been away at all. But Sheridan, an only child whose parents had died before he was five years old, could not return to what he'd hardly had. He had spent the rest of his childhood disclaiming persons who had claimed him. Thus his fantasy, beneath which ran so strong an undertow of desire for what he fantasied that times were when he drifted thoughtfully back to his childhood not knowing what was real and what was not.

So it was one afternoon in a hotel room in Paris where he had been sitting drinking alone. His window swung open in the wind and let up sounds from the street so close, so planted with the signposts of nostalgia, that the traffic appeared to have detoured three stories up from the Rue du Bac and to be going home across his lips. It was six o'clock in the evening.

Lights had been on; stars came out. Stars fell in and out of chimney pots, but this frequently happened, so it did not bother him. What was bothersome were the cities on the rug at his feet. Three pieces gleaming in various kinds of light. Three American places jazzing softly away: We'll have Manhattan, the Bronx, and Staten Island too. And smelling: how could frying potatoes fry so sad? How could it be so bad to forget, not really forget, but to get lost going back to the Cool Place, Temple Place, place of marble and glass? There, the spouts were gold, I swear. There lay ribbons on the air where the G&E fan had put them. Red and white and blue.

Who were they?—were they really?—who sat in white together on the moon-round stools gaily refusing the fact that consumption—It must have been—it was, and not a cough, a tickle, a "fine how do you do, Jim Sheridan, when you won't even take what the doctor . . ." Where was it? *I*? Just as that which had been mounting lighted in the sky broke like a bowl full of candles and dripped oozing into mouths Ahhh—and went out, leaving two black laughter-lined holes where they'd been talking, touching, I-love-you-ing beneath the ribbons? Holes in a drugstore into which he thrust searching lights on the Fourth of July, the first of his birthdays he remembered.

Sheridan was surprised sometimes that he had become thirty with only Saint Anthony to help him take thirty-one and all the rest, the thought of which hung up inside him, momentary pendants of despair. God he believed in, not because he thought He was everywhere, but because he hoped He was. He hoped he was in the right place always, Sheridan did; but the corners of his eyes, like the gambler's back door, never locked themselves closed to the fact of escape: Wasn't he in the right place now?

Swallowing this reluctant thought, the turnstile of his

mind clicked: he stood looking at the sisters with the withdrawn look of a man listening to war news.

"Isn't it too late?" he said to the sister who had addressed him.

She replied that it was not so late.

"Thank you."

"You are welcome."

They all four sat quietly then, Sheridan drinking wine, and the sisters smoking. After awhile, when all the restlessness had run out of the air and you could hear the trees beyond the ticking of the bead curtain, the eldest of the sisters, and the hardiest one, obviously, stamped out her cigarette and began to talk.

"You were here before, one year. Last year? Yes, last year with a large man whose manner was violent though I considered him kind. His name?"

"Yes," Sheridan replied, "last year. Kind, though violent: Cooper."

"Yes, Cooper. It was last year during the American suicides; one from a hospital window. I am interested in why Americans jump from windows and bridges. Is it because there is no one to talk to? My sisters tell me questions like that are for men to ask of other men; but I have found through experience that my brain is equal to the brains of most men."

"I'm sure it is," Sheridan told her.

"Yes. I think sometimes I have the brain of a man, and the body—such as it is—of a woman. Look! My sisters are outraged. Would you think that I alone of the three of us have known a man?"

"You were married then?"

"Yes, but he is dead, naturally."

"When?"

"After his father."

"When was that, Signora?"

"During the electricity. He depressed himself to death with the electricity, because he did not like electricity, naturally, but improvement; and these are no improvement, these things. One cannot be as proud of the café when these go on as when the beautiful gas went on. Are you from New York?"

"In a way, yes."

"I would not like it; but Rome I do. I have seen Rome. Also, I have been to Venice and Florence besides Rome, but I do not count them. What have you seen?"

He told her he liked Paris most of the cities.

"Well, Paris, yes. But I would not like New York. During Mussolini we were told we would not. That was very tiresome, being told. You do not like it here. That's a pity."

"No, I like it."

"Cooper did not like it, but he has come back."

The Macaroni

"No. He will not come."

"Yes. He has come, Signor Sherry."

The curtains clashed. Cooper, who was big and well dressed, and getting fat, crossed the café with his hand out to the eldest sister, who took it rather warmly. They exchanged greetings, and then Cooper took the hands of her sisters and they exchanged greetings.

"You have just arrived from Naples?" the eldest sister asked.

"Not just, but from Naples, yes; this afternoon. I am staying in Corvo."

"Corvo has bigger hotels."

"Yes. May I have something?"

"It's too late, Coop," Sheridan said.

Cooper was the kind of person who picks up a chair full from the floor and puts it down almost in the same place again before sitting on it. He did this now before he sat and faced Sheridan.

"You've come in the night on fog-feet like the cat, Coop," said Sheridan.

"No, I've been here all day. Did you have a good boat-ride? I heard you nearly drowned, but I couldn't hope. You'll never drown, will you?"

"Maybe. I hate water."

"Could you tell me why the hell you did not meet me in

Corvo? Of course I knew you'd come back to Rome sometime—if only for money. Still, I was curious. *Was.*"

"It's too nice a night, Coop. —Matter of fact I did start out . . . !"

"But I forgot: all my hate's gone, Sherry. I feel cold as the moon. An ant would die in a walk across my hand right now, you know that?"

"I know Albert Schweitzer drops drops of water down for his ants in Africa to drink."

"Sherry, remember the night we hired motorcycles and raced each other up to Montmartre. It was after the fortuneteller told you for fifty cents that you shouldn't ever live by the sea."

"Coop, remember how you kept yelling, 'Stay by me away from the sea,' and I kept saying, 'Stay by you? You're doom number two'?"

"She never said anything about me."

"No? She asked who you were, and when I said you were my friend, she closed her eyes, remember? and shook her head, and moaned, 'Move in from the sea, move in from the sea.'"

"I liked the balloons in Messina: yellow and red like Spain, remember? Remember how we bought them all just as the little bronze people came out of the clock, and let them go when the bells rang? It was twelve o'clock noon, wasn't it? I like this résumé. I'm very mellow, Sherry. What about you?"

"I'm only a little sad. Did you see Billy Helion?"

"Yes. He told me you went off with a woman. I sent him home."

"No, he's outside. Billy's always outside."

The eldest sister got up and went to the door and called someone, one of the Americans who had been there earlier around the table Mrs. Markham had studied.

"I was worried as to your respective healths," he said, coming in.

"Billy," said Cooper, "you're as newsy as grass. Go home."

"I think you all better stop being sonsabitches and let these women close up."

"There are not many things better than conversation, Signor Helion," said the eldest sister, "even that which it grieves me to hear, though I do not understand what it is that's being said. Please sit down."

She turned on her sisters and ordered them to bed.

"This is a fly-mark of a town," she said, after her sisters had gone, "but I only mind it when these two, resenting the outside world, show they would like it to be less of a fly-mark than it already is. They are very provincial. There is a man here, Frederico Siligato is his name, who is a veteran of three wars, though he looks more like the wife of a soldier. Still, he has been to all those wars; and me? I have seen Rome."

Sheridan reminded her that she had also seen Venice.

"Yes, Venice. But Venice is not a city: all that water! And death seems always to be reaching for one's hand. I was bored there, because I knew I would not die, and I loathe being teased."

"Sherry," said Cooper, "remember the Senegalese nigger with the fur-lined parka? You wouldn't let him take off his drawers because you said you could see the dirt on them, but you were worried about the dirt we couldn't see on him. You were always a nasty little stickler about soap and water."

"Water again! It's beginning to feel damp as the inside of a baptismal fount: mine was very high, Billy. It stood beside a mountain of lace—Rose Weinstein, my godmother."

"Don't you think Billy should go home, Sherry? I think so. I think he should go home and tell his mother she wants him."

"But she's always wanted me!" cried Billy. "Why don't you two turn off the gas under your fat tongues and leave this poor thing close up? We can go to my place."

"Look, Helion," said Cooper. "I've just come from your place. I don't want to go back and be alone with you and my friend in your place. Besides I don't like your place.

The Macaroni

You'll excuse us, Signora: it's not so late, is it?"

"No, it is not so late."

"I will tell a funny story then," said Cooper. "It is about myself, Sherry, and my car. I had a car then because my father was very rich, as rich, indeed, as he is today; but that was before my little book which so outraged him, my father, that he cut my money, and now I have nothing. No car, no money, no friend. Isn't this funny?"

"Busting," said Billy.

"Well, one night in Rome I had parked somewhere in the car when some police came by, bored. They asked me for my passport, my *permesso di soggiorno*, everything. I had nothing. So the police arrested me. I sent them to our apartment to Sherry, who said he did not know me. 'No, never heard of—Cooper, did you say?' I spent one whole night, no almost forty-eight hours in jail, Signora. And when I came home eventually and Sherry held out his hand smiling to me, I bit it. Show the scar, Sherry."

"Ha!" the eldest sister laughed. "I am recalled to the time I snatched at the head of an enemy of mine, and she ran off leaving me with a great long handful of her hair. Scalped! I thought, and that was the only time I fainted."

"But how wonderful, Signora," said Cooper, who really thought so.

"We must go now, Signora," said Helion. "It is late."

"Yes, there is no cheer left in the night. Look at this electricity! I would not make a decision now if my life depended on it. Good night."

"You have been very kind, Signora," Sheridan said to her at the door.

"It is nothing. It is as easy to be kind as it is to comb your own hair. Good night."

"You will close up now and go to bed?" Helion asked her.

"Of course I will go to bed," she replied. "I have led a full life."

"She has a very large screw loose in her little head, don't you think, Billy?" Cooper said as they crossed the piazza.

"No," Billy replied.

"No? Are you crazzy, or is it island pride?"

"I hate to see people break up, I mean," said Billy. "I knew a woman who spent her summers breaking up dogs. She was a miserable woman. I hope two are on her grave this minute."

"You can leave us now, Billy," Cooper told him. "Sherry knows the way to his *pensione,* and I know the way to Corvo. Good night, Billy. I'll write you from Rome."

"You can't walk to Corvo."

"Yes I can."

"No you can't, you slob. You're drunk and resentful that

you've said so much and came so far to say it. The trouble with you is you haven't got the nerve to go back on all you've said, which you should, and which you'll do in Rome anyway."

Sheridan, who had climbed the step to the *pensione* and had already inserted the key in the lock, withdrew it and came back into the street. He walked past both young men.

"Come on, Coop," he said, "I'll walk you a way."

Leaving Helion, they walked a way together up the road beside the sea and the mountain to the little powerhouse which furnished electric light to the town. Here, Cooper stopped and started talking, but nothing he said could be heard over the pounding machinery. They walked on. Sheridan said:

"The island looked all bent over and still like the shoulders of Mary Magdalen at the foot of the cross: I swam in from the boat. You seem very drunk, Coop, are you?"

"I'm glad you like it here, Sherry. No."

"I hate it here."

"No, you like it. You can't begin by hating it, Sherry. You must come to that slowly, with dignity. Wait till you get the feeling of being stuck."

"I couldn't be stuck, Coop."

"You've never waited for anything but money, have you?"

Friends and Vague Lovers

"What a nervous good-by you're making, Coop."

"I'm not nervous, Sheridan."

In the bay there was a small lighted steamboat which in a few hours would leave for Naples.

"I don't know why you don't wait and take that," Sheridan said, pointing to it.

"Write me, Sherry, for the sake of old times."

They no sooner parted than they turned, each with his hands in his pockets, and faced each other smiling uneasy smiles. A parade of early light passed between them. Light so marked the ground that the pebbles appeared as ancient cities fallen again in miniature, ruts in the road were baths for Montezuma one might now fill with a little spit. Rustlings of loneliness trailed lizards up walls; a rooster crowed.

"The day's calling card," said Cooper, pointing self-consciously at the air as though a hole had been torn in it, and at still another as the rooster crowed again.

"Coop, is that a morning I see shining through us summers from now? If it is, we're nicer as grass."

"Much nicer, Sherry. See you then."

Again the rooster crowed, and again and again; but you could still hear Cooper breathing as he climbed away up the hill. He hated to walk.

The Macaroni

When Sheridan returned to the *pensione*, Billy Helion rose from the step where he'd been sitting waiting.

"I don't know whether it feels like an operating table, or a cold-water flat on a winter morning. —Come up to my place, Sherry."

"There's a piece of sand got caught between what was and what is, Billy. I can't see you from looking. Go away!"

"Sand is so remindful. —Don't go in there."

"Please, Billy. You're as tiresome as a comeback."

"I know," replied Billy. "Why am I so vicariously everybody's, when I really don't give a damn? —It's so like a friend of mine's cold-water flat this morning, it's to die! —Why do I do it, Sherry?"

"Your soul's been out too late and is wanting its bedclothes, Billy Helion. You know, Cooper's never forgiven me for not being an artist."

"You don't care about that."

"No. Good night. Let me go unscrew these crossed rifles from my heart, and put whatever's carrying my tongue around my head to sleep with aspirin. There! It's gone: Baby's awake now, Billy! Baby *is* awake!"

[*Chapter Five*]

Mrs. Markham thought it remarkable.

"One would never know such things went on here," she said, looking steadily for a moment at the ice-blue walls, and at the people leaning against them holding martini glasses, which were, for the most part, empty. Then she looked into her own glass, which was full.

"Such things don't really," Billy Helion told her. "It's just a way of warding off Easter; though Easter's past, isn't it?"

"A party, yes," said Mrs. Markham, which was exactly what she feared it was not. Yet, it had sounded gay from downstairs when Sheridan had shown her the kitchen:

what an extraordinary name the young man had who had interrupted them.

"Those awful dyed eggs!" said Helion. "Did you ever do them when you were little?"

"Others did," Mrs. Markham replied seriously, "but I was too stern. As I remember us, though, we were all stern, stern and stiff like figures in a sampler."

"Have you known Sherry long, Mrs. Markham?"

"Not long, no. He was a friend of my son's."

Moving, Mrs. Markham spilled a little of her drink on her coat. It was too chilly in the unheated rooms for her to take the coat off. The kitchen certainly had been much the warmer place, but the young man had insisted, rightly, perhaps, that they come join the party.

"Is he really called Hallelujah?" she asked Helion, who looked up sharply, she thought, from the spot on her coat which he was wiping with his handkerchief.

"Who? Yes, he lives here too. Haller's his last name."

"Just the two of you live here?"

"When we can manage it, yes. Unless the boat from Naples brings a friend."

"You mean more Macaroni, as Sheridan calls, I suppose, all of you?"

"As Haller does, Mrs. Markham," Helion corrected her.

"Haller? The one called Hallelujah? Well, actually, it belongs to neither of them. It was used in the eighteenth century to designate rather precious travelers, young men, naturally, who affected foreign ways. You see I've looked it up."

"There's more of Haller in the next room," said Helion. "Would you care to see it?"

Mrs. Markham replied that she would. "But I must take care," she said, getting up, "not to spill this again."

In the next room there were also more people. Haller's paintings stood on the floor in the corner, below one which had been hung. "It's hardly a good time to see it," said Helion.

"Billy seems to be at a loss to know what to say to your lady friend, Sherry," said a young man whose face was serene and priestly pale. "Hates my paintings, poor Billy does."

"Oh, come off it, Haller," said a scrunched-faced woman called Mrs. Christophe.

"No, it's true," said Haller. "It hasn't anything to do with their being good or bad; it's simply that Billy considers almost all endeavor a fraud."

Poor Billy is right, thought Mrs. Christophe, who also painted. They really are awful. "But I liked a show of yours I saw before the war, Haller," she said. "Didn't we, Chris?" she called across the room to her husband. "Don't you remember us saying we *liked* Haller's stuff?"

Haller drew Sheridan aside:

Friends and Vague Lovers

"Aren't you pleased to see the Christophes, Sherry? How she could have left Fifty-seventh Street for one moment is beyond me. I found her racing through my new paintings when I came up from the kitchen with you."

"What are they doing here?"

"They've come to sell their souls to the devil, but can't find him. Could you help them, I wonder now, Sherry?"

"To find the devil, Haller? Are you trying to drive me home?"

"Could you, Sherry?"

"Could I what?"

"Go to what you haven't got.—*Don't* move toward the door. There's something strange wedged in it and won't come out.—Yes, home."

"You're depressing me a little, Haller. Who is he, anyway, in the doorway. He's been standing, and standing."

"Like you, Sherry. It's true, he's afraid to come in, and you're afraid to sit down. Has that woman frightened you?"

"Mrs. Markham? You've met her."

"Yes. But about the boy in the doorway—I don't know him. He came in from Corvo with the Christophes, who, by the way, have taken to calling each other Chris. He brought along a letter of introduction, which seemed to hurt him to show. Name's Crystal. Made up, don't you think?"

The Macaroni

"But why does he hang in the doorway?—Oh, I don't care. Go talk to someone else, Haller."

"Because—Yes you do—for him to come into a room means to give himself away. Someday somebody will tell him he's nobody, or he'll just find out for himself. Actually, he's all right, if only because he doesn't mean to stay, but is bound for Africa. Come meet him."

"But it isn't the way, is it, really, to Africa?" said Sheridan, walking toward the boy in the doorway and speaking to him. The boy rubbed his hand over his face, which was dark, and rather like a beautiful yellow-brown monkey's. He was small, and undoubtedly older than he appeared to be. For he seemed, at first sight, to be withholding not merely his smile, which the young often willfully do out of fear of committing themselves, but also a perfect good nature.

"He says," said Haller, "that this is hardly the way to Africa."

"Yes, I know," said Crystal. "But I was in Naples, and so I figured I'd come here and see what was doing."

"Let's go out on the terrace," said Haller. "It's not so cold, I don't think."

"No," said Crystal, "it's not. I was out there."

They went out through the room to the terrace and closed the door.

Mrs. Christophe, whose face ran all over her face, as

it were, scrunched it hard at Helion after Crystal had passed them: "How many can Africa take? Crazies, I mean, Billy. Why, as I said to Jennie Hornblow, you can die of exhaustion trying to keep out of people's way anywhere, Jennie; so why Africa? You know she's taken her husbands there, three now; because Jennie's divorces have a way of not coming through in time. Anyway, they live in Africa in a house without chairs. Jennie Hornblow living in sin in a house in Africa without chairs. It's too divine!"

"So he is going to Africa," said Helion. "I don't like him, do you?"

Mrs. Christophe leaned very close to Helion. She closed one eye, hid the corner of her mouth in her cheek, nodded and ducked so violently that her hair slipped from her red wool cap and whipped across Helion's face. "I like him, yes," she said, "but, as I said to Chris, why Africa? *Why Africa, Chris?"* Mrs. Christophe shouted across the room to her husband, who was talking with Mrs. Markham.

"Come see the twilight," said Helion, "there's a terrace."

"Come see the twilight, Chris," Mrs. Christophe shouted smack into the door Billy had opened for her. "I *see,* it opens in, doesn't it?" And once more she cried to Christophe, "Twilight, Chris!" for she was pushed into it by Billy Helion.

"Twilight in Turkey," said Mr. Christophe to Mrs. Markham, "is all I know of Turkey. Which reminds me, we came here to hear records. Is it feeling so, you think, or thinking so that makes the world's size for us, Mrs. Markham?"

"I think I feel about it," replied Mrs. Markham, "though I do know my geography. You see I used to teach school. Did you ever teach school, Mr. Christophe?" she asked, for that's the kind of conversation it was.

No, Mr. Christophe had not. He was a man nearing forty who might have passed for twenty. He was un-wrinkled as a tennis ball. It was said that his signs of coming of age—little pieces of dropsical flesh about the eyes and jaw, those deep wrinkles banding the neck, had all been taken over for him by poor Mrs. Christophe. For, if he had none, she had more than her due; and what she had, she tripled with her inspired grimacing.

She was a painter, and he a poet who had won prizes. And while he soared, though never so high that he could not be reached for supper, Mrs. Christophe scraped away at her easel and scoured New York in search of commissions. She was as well known to the art dealers on Fifty-seventh Street as the mounted policeman's horse, and was held, perhaps, in similar regard. For though she did her job well, people spent most of their time keeping out of her way.

"We're having a wonderful time," said Mr. Christophe, "but we're not here to stay, naturally." Mrs. Markham had said that she was. "It's all very well racing around museums, but one should always plan to get back." Mr. Christophe pointed his smooth chin sideways at Haller's paintings. "You have seen them, haven't you? Terrible, I think, how he's fallen off. Pity, too, because he's rather extraordinary, Haller; had a leg shot off in the war; but you wouldn't know it, would you?" Mrs. Markham said no, she didn't think she would. "Not enough stimulus," said Mr. Christophe. "No, not nearly enough. After all, what Henry James said to Edith Wharton still holds true."

Would he tell her—Mrs. Markham hoped not—what Henry James had said to——? Goodness! She hadn't heard that name in years. She hoped he would not, for the others were crowded darkly against the glass door like children, and she wanted desperately to hear what they had to say as they came in. "You can see a trace of limp now," said Mr. Christophe. "Night air, probably." "Would you put this down for me," said Mrs. Markham. He took her glass and put it down. And there!

They had come in.

"But let me finish, Haller!" Mrs. Christophe was saying. "I've said, and you know perfectly well that I do, Sherry, that I adore Cooper. But his enthusiasms leave me cold; cold as mine leave other people, I don't doubt. As a writer, he's about as objective as a dog with a bone."

"Or a bone-on," said Haller.

[78]

"Exactly. God! I haven't heard that quainty in years. He writes with spread legs, and doesn't know—Please, Haller, no more obscenities!—that it's laughter, and not an erection, that's our divinest thing. What a frowner he is, that Cooper."

Mrs. Markham supposed that they were not going to turn on lights.

"Who is Cooper?" she asked Mr. Christophe.

"Cooper," he replied, "is, or was, a friend of Sheridan's: they had a row. Cooper was here. We met him in Corvo, where we're staying."

"He was here, Cooper?"

"Yes, but he's gone back to Rome. Pity, too, because the other one rather depends on him."

Mrs. Markham and Mr. Christophe sat quietly blinking at candles going on across the room. Clusters of people stood silently against the blue walls watching Sheridan and Mrs. Christophe, each with a lighted match, going from candle to candle. They had been talking quietly and you would not have heard them in the general talk, but now you could, simply because everyone else was still.

"So we've been, Haller and I, friends ever since," Sheridan was saying. "Friends and vague lovers, in the way that friends are often lovers, whereas lovers are seldom friends."

"Friends and vague lovers," said Mrs. Christophe, who was kneeling. "How nice of you, Sherry, to think to light them." She put out her hand behind her. "Chris," she softly called, "Chris, where are you, my dearest?"

"Here I am, Chris," replied Mr. Christophe, who was sitting alone, for Mrs. Markham had gone.

She had gone so softly that no one had noticed. She had left swiftly, but had stepped into the kitchen below to linger for a moment where the party had begun for her, and where it had ended. Never was Sheridan so remote to her as he was now; never so beautiful as when he had bent to light the candles, which, coming on one by one by one, had counseled her to be wise and look away, to be wiser still and go.

She had climbed to desire, only to look on the worm of unfulfillment. It was a pity that at this late date in her life there could not be gratification, but there could not be. For what she wanted, after all, was that someone should sit still while she fed on him; someone that each day must face up to her inevitable jealousies, whose every step would be a crime because he could not, unless he walked backwards, keep step with her.

She was in love.

Sheridan had opened her up and she loved and hated him for doing so. She hated him for having destroyed her uneasy peace, and for having taken away her ability to enjoy anything except through him. She was too old, too disappointed to be dictated to; much too old to love again. Yet here she was in love.

She wanted to know if he did his teeth before retiring; and how many ties hung in his closet. She wanted to see him wash himself, and to see him comb his hair. Bliss it would be to see his shirts lying flat in a drawer, his ties making a mute holiday of colors in a closet. She wanted to bend over his things and learn them. Could she not give him gifts? she wondered. For the bridge between them was no bridge really, but only half a one coming from her. Like the fisherman's line, it played itself out in the passing current and caught nothing.

Distracted by these flashes of self-knowledge that come to us whether we will them or not, Mrs. Markham, loitering in a cold, strange, foreign kitchen, began to speak aloud to herself. "It's all very well for you to come in asking if I'm cold. Yes, I am cold." She took up the poker from the top of the stove, and held it rather like a pointer. "But what can you do for me? Or I for you? Aren't we weaving, you and I, something as carefully as these Italian women sitting in their doorways weave sewing baskets?"

"Mrs. Markham, Mrs. Markham," Sheridan called down the stairs. He was down and into the kitchen before Mrs. Markham had time to put away the poker. "You were cold up there, weren't you?" he asked.

"I was cold, yes."

Friends and Vague Lovers

There was light from the stone hallway, but Mrs. Markham kept out of it.

"That's the first time you've done that," she said, meaning Sheridan had sat down. "I was watching you up there, and——! *No!*" she exclaimed bitterly, for her hands and her heart were full and he could not see they were full. "No, I was not cold, nor am I now. I could not help thinking up there, seeing you so adored, that Jonathan never was, except by me. No—don't say anything, please. He loved you, didn't he? Jonathan loved you. Oh, I know how he must have loved you."

"Did he?" Sheridan asked her. "And if he did, did I choose him? I don't know. All I do know is that we used to meet in as anonymous a place as Providence, Rhode Island, and take buses to even more anonymous places. Years have passed since then, Mrs. Markham, or at least years of war, which is the same thing, and it's this you seem to forget."

"*Forget?* You've unburied my dead for me and now you tell me I forget!"

"I tell you I have my own dead!" Sheridan cried, "and I don't want them any more than you do yours."

"Only Billy sent me," said Haller, who came so softly into the kitchen that both Mrs. Markham and Sheridan wondered which they had heard first, his steps, or his voice. He limped into the light and out of it, and all around the

[82]

kitchen, before he spoke again. "Billy says to come up, Sherry, because he's playing your favorites. He isn't, of course. He's simply playing at people again, worried that you might be having a better time than he is. It's the kitchen too, you see, because he's altogether mystic about kitchens: says they always look like morning to him."

"Mourning?" said Mrs. Markham. "How odd."

"The beginning of the day, I mean," said Haller. "Were you making a fire?"

"We were doing," said Sheridan angrily, "what our hosts might have done for us. Yes, we were building a fire, do you mind, Hallelujah?"

Haller accompanied them into the hall.

"God must keep you, Sheridan," he called down the stone steps after them. "Do you know why?"

Ignoring him, Sheridan said, "I hope we can still get our dinner, Mrs. Markham."

". . . Because," Haller shouted savagely, "the devil has given you up."

The phonograph began to play piano music, which made people look up at the closed windows as they passed. Mrs. Markham said, "They might have done that before, don't you think, Sheridan?"

At the *pensione,* Sheridan asked Antonia if anything had come for him during his absence.

"Anything, Signor Sheridan? You mean your friend?"

"Cooper? Is *he* here?"

"No, no, Signor; but there could not be letters, and there is no telephone, so I thought you meant your friend. No, nothing came, no friend."

"Of course nothing could have come," said Mrs. Markham impatiently. "Don't you realize it's Sunday?"

"Yes, I'd forgotten. It is Sunday, isn't it?"

As Mrs. Markham entered the dining room she burst into laughter. "It's the way that poor child looked at us. Didn't you notice? Why it was as though she thought we were trying, between the two of us, to frighten her to death."

"Strange," said Haller, blowing out what little of the candles there still remained from the party, "that those two should have been the ones to make that special kind of extra-party atmosphere. I mean their being discovered off in the kitchen together."

Annoyed, Helion said, "You mean you entered a room where two people were talking together, and that makes a discovery?"

"Yes. I dislike her. She's playing with fire, and out to burn everything in sight."

"How do you know?"

The Macaroni

"Because I'm bright," Haller replied wearily.

"Oh you think . . . !"

"Precisely, and you don't. That woman knows what she wants. That tearful eye she has on her past is only an eye in a dream. You'll see, she'll be with Sheridan constantly; because now that he knows her, he'll need her."

Helion, wondering if that applied in their case to Crystal, said, "You've just got your usual wild concern about Sheridan. And *don't* step into the wax he's let drip everywhere. Christ! I could be on fire and nobody would give a damn, least of all you."

"That's because you wouldn't burn through, Billy. Sherry will."

"Please forgive us for leaving the confessional open, Crystal," said Helion, loathing him. "You see, Father Haller's had a bad day."

Crystal, who was sitting on the bowlegged sofa Mrs. Markham and Mr. Christophe had occupied, said, without smiling, that he would. The Christophes came up from the kitchen then; and Billy bent with a knife to the floor to scrape up the wax that had melted off the candles. Accompanying the Christophes was a tall, thin young man who said that everything made him ill. "All of it makes me sick, good and damned sick and tired." No one asked what the matter was, so he went to the corner of the room and

[85]

made faces at Haller's painting. "That makes me awful sick," he said. He sat down beside Crystal and went to sleep.

"Imagine getting drunk at a party like this was," said Helion, pointing his knife at the sleeper. "Does anybody know him?"

"I think," said Mrs. Christophe, "that he left a motorcycle in Amalfi, or somewhere. No, we don't know him."

"Well, take him with you to Corvo, will you, please."

"Will he like that? Wake him, Chris. He's a student of aeronautics. I'm suddenly tired. Let's go."

Mr. Christophe looked tired too as he bent over the young man. Next to the young man's face, Mr. Christophe's face was old as it was. "We're going to Arezzo," he said, lifting the young man to his feet. "We've practically come to Europe to see the Pieros, so we must get to Arezzo."

Everyone but Crystal appeared disgruntled.

"Well, it's been lovely, hasn't it, Chris?" said Mrs. Christophe, remembering that there had been a party.

"Yes," said Haller. "We won't go out with you. Do you mind? Good-by."

"Not at all," said Mrs. Christophe. "And thanks for the drinks. Lovely time, dolls. Love your place."

"Oh yes. Thanks," said Mr. Christophe. "Wonderful time, really."

The Macaroni

They watched Mr. Christophe from the window running after a carriage. Mrs. Christophe struggled along, supporting the aeronautics student who had left his motorcycle in Amalfi.

Haller walked away from the window followed closely by Helion. "I was saying," he said, "that Sheridan's a darling. Strange, too, because precious as he is, that's all he is. I wish he'd go away. Something's happening to him that we shouldn't want to see."

"Please get off the wax."

"You're not listening to me, Billy. Get off what wax?"

"You're standing on my pile of wax, goddammit!"

"Listen, Haller," said Crystal, "why doesn't that guy come to Africa with me?"

"Because he hasn't the money," snapped Helion. He gave Haller the knife. "You get the rest of that crap up. I'm going to fix us some supper."

"What is there, Billy?" Haller asked, slipping the knife absent-mindedly into his back pocket. "Shall we help?"

"No. Stay up here. I'll call *you* when I'm ready."

Crystal sat for awhile with his chin resting on his knees after Helion had gone down to the kitchen. Then he began talking excitedly to Haller.

"You see, this is what I don't want!"

"What are you talking about? I thought it was quite pleasant."

"Well, it wasn't," said Crystal. "It's been nervous, jealous, tight, tired, and—escapey."

"Escapey?"

"Yes. Dig me, for Christ's sake, Haller! You all escaped so far, I mean, but not far enough."

Haller felt vaguely complimented at being confided in, but he was annoyed that Crystal did not make a distinction between himself and others. He would have preferred being told he had escaped more, or less, rather than precisely as 'the others' had.

"I'm not aware," he said, "that we have escaped anything, or that we can. Where are you from?"

"Oh, take a piece of any dirty city," said Crystal; "take Youngstown, Pittsburgh, or Detroit; take smoke and steel and fires that haven't the decency to go out and let you sleep; take a candy store with spit on the floor; take an old guy with a cigarette built permanently into his face; take me, for instance . . . ! What's it matter where I come from?"

"A great deal," replied Haller. "Because it's still with you, and it will stay with you till you make peace with it. You don't want to lose anything for awhile, perhaps, but the fact that you're from Detroit, and that your old man picked his teeth and nose after dinner."

"In his undershirt on the front steps," Crystal broke in with a smile. He put down his knees and took one of

The Macaroni

Haller's cigarettes and showed that he was not terribly used to smoking. He sat smoking and thinking, and his face cleared and softened. "Things have always been happening to me like messages. Do you want to hear about one of these experiences of mine, Haller?"

"Yes," said Haller, "but hold it just a minute while I go see about food."

When Haller returned, Crystal put his cigarette out and asked for another.

"What kind are they, Italian?"

"Italian, yes. They're called Nazionalis. Do you like them?"

"Yes. It's nice of you to invite me to dinner. I hadn't thought——"

"You were about to say something," said Haller.

"I know. Well, I've lived in New York since the war, in a cold-water flat. When I left, I took a taxi down Second Avenue. I had all I have: two duffel bags. It was a hot day, but it was February. The sun was hot. I think it was a Friday. At the bridge at Fifty-ninth Street a lady was sitting on the curb with a cop standing next to her. There was something funny about her face, so that I didn't want to look at her, but I did. I didn't want to look at her because I felt she was doing something very personal, like dying. Her face was gray. She was scared, but hid it, or tried. Like if she was going to die right there, she was going to die right. Under where she sat there was blood. There was blood down her legs, and a puddle of it between her feet in the curb. Her hat was on; and she didn't let go of her pocketbook, not for as long as I saw her, anyway, which wasn't long."

"A vertical moment deepens with time," said Haller. "Whereas most moments stretch out horizontally."

"What? Yes. But don't you see that she was bleeding to death with her hat on, and holding her pocketbook with the law standing beside her? Don't you see everybody was involved? Don't you feel that it was America?"

"Here's Billy," said Haller.

"No, it's me," said Sheridan. "Billy told me to tell you both to go down. It's fish. Look, you've blown out the party candles, haven't you, Haller? I had a schoolteacher named Rose Coughlin who gave me a plant to keep for her every summer. None died, because they were Rose's— But wait. Before you go down let me tell you what Rose Coughlin said. She asked me what I did before I went to bed. I told her that right before I went to bed I turned out the light. 'Do you,' she said, 'put the light out carefully, so it won't spill over into the dark and keep you awake?' I said I didn't know, but I hoped I did. Then Rose Coughlin said, 'I know you do, and I hope you always do.' Now you can go. I'll be waiting."

[*Chapter Six*]

MOONLIGHT GOES to the bone and puts the flesh to sleep. Crystal's voice appeared to die as it left his lips, and to be reborn again in the air between himself and Haller. Sheridan stood apart from them in the propitiatory shadow of the church, resting his hands on the stone parapet. The sea was silvered where it was not black. It was still as a meadow out where the fishing boats were. From the boats the bastioned church might have looked like a fantastic chocolate with its creamy center showing.

White and heavy-bottomed as a dove, the church had no little door cut out of its right big one, which was as consoling to Sheridan, somehow, as the fact that when he tried it, the great wooden door opened. There was no vestibule. Moonlight shot obliquely across the stone floor to a candle rack whose outlines were swollen by a fall of wax. Above it hung a dusty collection of small, curiously unframed paintings. The rest of the church was cave-dark; secret as the folds in an old woman's apron.

Sheridan, lighting a candle which he took from a box of them attached to the rack, held it up to the pictures. But the moonlight, pressing the shadow out of substance, the substance out of shadow, wrestled the candle's flame down and almost out. Reaching again into the box, Sheridan took from it what candles remained—about five; these he lit and held up as one to the pictures.

The pictures showed the world of the sea under stress.

As Sheridan looked at them his excitement mounted as the waves in the unframed paintings mounted. Waves like watery mouths opened wide, foaming with teeth; waves like cabbages, men like worms; men trying to kneel on the waves. The paintings had a curious reality in that God should have appeared in all, but he appeared in none. One did not know if they had been painted by a recluse who had never been to sea, or by a fisherman-artist who had been, and who had not found it in his heart to put into the paintings anything that his flooded eyes had not actually seen.

The Macaroni

A rod of light imbedding an old, thin priest made a tear, suddenly, in the dark at the front of the church. He glided forward sucking his teeth into place.

"Can I help you?" he asked Sheridan.

Sheridan moved his flaming candelabra down from the pictures.

"As a matter of fact," he replied. "I'm looking for Saint Anthony. Is he here?"

The old priest turned as another priest hurried out over the fan of light at the front of the church. The new one was young. His face came to an effectual point at his nose, like a rat's. Small as his eyes were, they managed to contain the question, "Have you *paid* for those candles?"

"What is wrong?" he asked, peeved.

"The young man is looking for San Antonio."

"A statue of San Antonio? No, there is none. No."

While the young priest's No reverberated throughout the little church by the sea, the old priest, half closing his eyes, began rapidly to enumerate the miracles of the saint in a husky, sick voice: "He restored a drowned woman to life. He healed a woman wounded by her husband. He reattached the foot of a young boy amputated after he had kicked his mother. He preached from a nutmeg tree. He was a very human one."

Sheridan paid the old priest for the candles and went

[93]

out, realizing only after he had done so that though he had
thought the church silent it had not actually been so. It
had contained the roar of the sea waves as a seashell does.

Crystal and Haller were still gesticulating in the moonlight like life-sized marionettes playing to an empty house.
A conical shadow hung from Crystal's lower lip. Haller's
face, more like a smiling mask than ever, appeared to be
depressingly in need of repair. Violent staccato shadows
wounded their faces as though each had been struck
through the cheeks with golf balls. "It's this horrible moonlight," said Haller. He touched his face as if he were
about to take it off. "Let's go down to the beach, if you
don't mind?"

"Yes, but I do," said Sheridan. "And anyway, Helion's
waiting at the café."

"That's why I prefer not to go there," said Haller.

On the beach, which was a half a mile down from the
church, and not one where you ever bathed, they sat in the
shadow of the cliff. Silence from other people made Haller
uncomfortable. He blamed Crystal's silence on Sheridan,
and felt the beginning of an alliance between them. Attempting then to rouse Crystal, and cut short what he considered Sheridan's sly domination of the boy, Haller spoke
teasingly of the processions they had witnessed during
Holy Week. "It's a pity, Crystal, that you missed them."

The Macaroni

Crystal shrugged his shoulders and glanced sideways at Sheridan. There was a molelike desperation about him; he did darting animal movements when he moved, and when he was still he was squirrel-still.

"You know," said Haller, "you look AWOL."

Crystal brightened. "I am AWOL."

"Yes," said Haller, "I thought so myself."

"You thought so!" Crystal cried, digging his heels down through the sand. "Who do you think you are, any of you are, anyway? You were never wounded, were you?"

"Not," replied Haller, "as often as you, I'm sure."

"There goes one," cried Sheridan, pointing at a shooting star. "Didn't anybody see it?"

Crystal peered fiercely through the dark at him.

"Three times," he said, looking back at Haller.

He drew his knees up to his chin and looked with despair down his thin legs. He had got into shorts, though actually it was still too cold after sundown to wear them. Haller, noticing how very white and stiff and new they were, considered they made Crystal more what he was, instead of less. They were at once a sign of escape and bondage.

"Are you," he asked seriously, "really without pleasure?"

"Almost," Crystal replied promptly. "But I know what I want. And I know where I'm going even if it is to a place where the sun makes men look like pieces of string. You talk about rich and poor, Haller, but that hasn't anything to do with it. Nothing. It's the moving stairway today for everybody; and I don't want any part of it. Kill me, they can, it's all the same to me. But they catch me first—maybe. It all depends on maybe, you'll say, Haller; but when hasn't it, and when won't it, really, and when shouldn't it be maybe?"

Pausing, he squinted suspiciously up and down the beach as though he heard mockery in the champagne fizzle of the foam.

"I'm talking too much," he said, "but let me. Don't turn off my radio, guys."

"You're too brazen with your heart," Sheridan told him coldly. "Don't you know that a heart's a burden? That God, knowing we'd always be borrowing or begging another's, or having another's thrust on us, said, 'One, and one only to a man.' You are too free and uneasy with yours. But go on."

"I feel," Crystal continued heedlessly, "that we're talking; that none of us has stopped talking for weeks. I want to tell you about myself *now*. To begin with, I was shot down in France. When I landed I was myself for the first time in my life, but I didn't know it. It was a frightening feeling, and it made me ashamed, secretly ashamed of myself for feeling the way I did. I hadn't been any more noticeably scared than the others, so why was I ashamed? I began to find out why I felt the way I did when I heard the others talk. What they didn't like, I found myself liking. What scared them, pleased me. But I pretended to agree with them. It was true we had nothing and were nothing and didn't know where we were. It was also true you should be scared and uneasy. So I went along with them, hiding what I was from myself and from them. I was ashamed, for instance, that I couldn't take our position —they always said *our position*—seriously. But I couldn't, because I saw it as a continuation of the way I'd always been. I mean that I was nothing, and that I had nothing— that instead of feeling smaller because of this, I was bigger, and would do more than I'd ever imagined I'd do. And if I did nothing—so what? It would still be me. Don't you see that knowing I was nothing made me something, something bigger than my fear of not telling, of not fitting in, of trying and failing to be one of the boys, who were, by far, always, since I've been a kid, more frightened, really, of reality than I'd been. *They* weren't faced with danger, but decision; and they didn't know how to make a decision. I did because I'd always been making them—decisions to hate, mostly. Being shot down didn't kill or near-kill those guys. What did, nearly, was the fact that they'd been separated from the outfit. I'd always been, but didn't know it till then. And when I did know it, I was free. I had reached myself."

"And then," said Sheridan, who felt the silence was a

hurting one, "then what happened to you?" He rolled over and cupped his face in his elbows and smelled the sand, which was, he thought smiling, what Billy Helion had said it was, remindful.

"Then," said Crystal, "I did get away from them with another guy, and we had a ball. We got in with some maquis, who were crazy but all right."

Haller, who was impressed by Crystal, pretended to himself to be looking forward to tomorrow when he would not be.

"When do you leave?" he asked.

"In a few days," Crystal replied, hesitantly. He stared at Haller as though he'd just awakened from a recurrent dream of some loathsome place. "You see," he explained, "I'm looking for somebody to come along with me."

At the café, Billy Helion was not listening to a serious person called John Harness talk about the theater in New York, which he declared to be in a very bad state indeed. He carried a book called *The Playwright as Thinker*, which he said was also bad, though its author not so bad when compared to All Those Others.

Billy sat making precise circles in the air with the toe of his right foot. John Harness said the dramatic school at the New School for Social Research was filled with young ladies running out on Twelfth Street to procure containers of coffee for other young ladies, who had parts. The young ladies who had been sent for coffee, which they frequently had to pay for, or half pay for, though they only tasted the coffee upon request, to see whether or not there was enough sugar, or no sugar, as the case might be, had no parts.

Billy yawned, and did his last circle with his right foot, then changed to his left. "Sit down, Sherry," he said. "We're talking about the theater."

"Have some *caffelatte*," said John Harness.

"You have been walking, Signor Sherry?" the eldest of the three sisters said in greeting from behind the bar.

"Good evening, Signora," Sheridan replied. "No, I have not been, really, because there is no place to walk. I have been to church."

"When I was a young girl I frequently went to church alone. That was before my marriage, naturally, and not since. Now I go with everybody, which is the way it should be."

John Harness said the ballet tended to supersede the drama in his interest, and that he did not wonder any longer why it should not. Speaking from a backstage point of view, he named dancers correctly, and ballet positions almost so. While Sheridan wondered if that wasn't Crystal passing outside in his deplorable Provincetown week-end shorts, John Harness vocally bemoaned the lack of financial support given to theatrical dancing in North America. He reported a company lost in *South* America.

"*Not*, I hope in a jungle?" said Billy, giving up his circles.

Harness, who usually listened solely to quotable celebrities and train-station announcements, looked blank for a second, then proceeded to tell how he had near died laughing at the opening night of a ballet called "Flowering Cactus." The people beside him, said John, had made him laugh even more, simply because they had not laughed at all. "Yes, I know," he replied abstractedly to Billy Helion, who also complained of near-dying at the ballet—any ballet.

As Sheridan, sure that it was Crystal outside, left the café, he heard Billy ask in a very loud voice, "Do you pronounce it J. M. *Singe, Sing, or Sin?*"

"Are you cold?" he asked Crystal.

"No. You know, I really don't get along with Haller."

"And do you know," Sheridan replied, laughing, "that *you* remind me of guys who think they can run the bases without ever hitting the ball?"

"I didn't know he had that leg. How . . . ?"

"Crocodile. Come up to my place and have a drink."

"A drink isn't what I want so much as to be quiet. It'll

be a mistake for me to go to Helion's. Are you going to sit up for awhile?"

"I don't know what I'm going to do," Sheridan answered, somewhat impatiently. "Come up if you like."

Crystal, trailing behind with an air of reluctance, followed Sheridan to the *pensione*. As they were about to enter Sheridan's room, the door next door opened, and Mrs. Markham appeared with a book opened in her hand. "I was wondering," she said, "what was the commotion."

"Was there commotion? We're going to talk. Would you care to come in for a nightcap? I don't know if you like it or not—some gin?"

"No, thank you, Sheridan. Yes, I do, but now, no. Weren't you," she addressed Crystal, "at the party?" Crystal replied that, yes, he had been; but had not had a chance to talk to her. "I might," said Mrs. Markham suddenly, "drop in a little later."

She withdrew into her room and closed the door.

"I don't much feel like talking," Sheridan said after they'd gone in.

"Well, that's all right," Crystal replied.

He moved busily around the room picking things up—postcards, books, snapshots—and putting them down without comment. Sheridan sat down on a stool at the foot of his bed. He looked the other way from Crystal, whose prying annoyed him, though he knew it was not really prying but a desire, perhaps, to nestle, or at least to sniff another's nest: a depressing, though typical, trait of the chance acquaintance, the passing traveler.

"Crystal," he said suddenly, as though an idea had just occurred to him, "do you like to undress people?" Keeping his face averted, it amused him to wonder, not what Crystal would answer, but what he was holding at that moment, what picture postcard, or book; holding it and not seeing it. Crystal, putting something noiselessly down, replied that he never had; but, "I'll try, if you want."

There was a knock on the door, which would have been at that moment impossible to answer.

Still, thoughts that rouse you from sleep are like gaudily arrayed strangers; strangers who insist they've met you before and know you quite as well as you know yourself. Facing them at two in the morning, not knowing if it had been the roar of the sea or simply thinking of the sea that had awakened him, Sheridan, sick with the fact he'd been wrong to leave Rome, wrong about Cooper, altogether wrong to be where he was, threw back the blankets to his feet and switched on a light.

Sitting up, he stared down at Crystal, who lay curled like an ear on his side at the head of the bed. After a few minutes which seemed endless to him, Sheridan reached around and took from the bedside table a pair of handcuffs, the one gift from Cooper he had with him. He tossed them down by Crystal, who, as they touched him, whimpered in his sleep. Opening his eyes so wide that they looked square, he asked warily, "What are you up to, anyway?"

"Just up. Up and wondering. I'm sorry, but—could you go?"

"Go where?"

"Oh, I don't care."

"I think," said Crystal, "that you feel like being alone?"

"Oh no. Not at all. I want to talk. I think you should talk to me. Look." He took up the handcuffs and gave them to Crystal. "You missed these."

"Missed them? Oh you mean when I was looking around the room. What are you doing with them?"

"Souvenir."

Crystal held the handcuffs close to his face and pretended to examine them.

"Does the sea sound extra loud to you now?" Sheridan asked.

"No. Why?"

"Nothing. I think I'm being sick. Do you mind if I throw you out? Maybe you don't hear as well as I do?"

". . . Maybe."

[103]

"You were so damned positive about everything else," Sheridan cried suddenly. "What's the matter with you now? *Answer me, are your ears all right or not?*"

"They're all right."

"And the sea's not noticeably loud?"

"Not noticeably."

Sheridan got up and stood listening at the shutter. "No, I wouldn't say it was."

"No, I don't think so," Crystal said, putting the hand-cuffs very quietly back on the table. "I think you were just awakened by it. Maybe the tide changed?"

"Maybe that was it. But I think you'd better go, don't you? I'm terribly annoyed with myself. Do you ever get that way?"

"Yes, often," Crystal replied. "But not in just your way. Why don't you come lie down?"

"Please go, will you?"

Crystal's feet sounded like hand claps striking the tiled floor. His face, as he bent to dress, drained to a blunt and heavy point at his mouth—itself so disfigured by a show of fear that it looked negroid. Watching him sorrowfully, Sheridan suggested he carry his shoes out with him.

There appeared to be next morning no point in getting up. Picturing with loathing the source of every sound he heard, Sheridan lay listening to donkeys, to roosters, and to Antonia and the proprietor's wife—all their noises blending into one lovesick Neapolitan song being played on a machine loud as it was old. Buses and carriages sped in and out of town past two women who screamed affectionately at each other in the street below.

Thoroughly exhausted finally by what was not actually present in his room, Sheridan opened his eyes to see what was: white wedding-cake roses in plaster relief above, a mobile bidet with black, reproachful legs across from him, and, surrounding him like a prison with its walls melted frighteningly away, his bed.

No one lived here. A valise, some clothing, a few books, indicated a traveler more anonymous, perhaps, than was the room, whose bleak periphery had been *occupied* during the night.

Denying anxiously to himself the effort it cost him to do so, Sheridan got up. He wavered beside the bed, attempting to reflect actively what a small, square, domestic-bright Flemish Interior part of himself told him, and, indeed, had been telling him for days, he *had* to do.

It had cost him no effort to get up, he told himself. Nothing ached in him. He was not tired. He *had* got up, after all. He *was* walking. And though everything was heavier than it had a reasonable right to be, he was gathering things up and putting them into his valise. His shirt, though dry, was as heavy as if it were soaking wet. Even the air seemed threaded with bubbles breaking against him. Still, he did feel all right. It was rather as if another person, not present, had risen from a bed, also not present; and that person, moving exactly as he, himself, Sheridan, moved, complained of the effort it cost him to do so.

To do anything? Sheridan wondered. Well, *almost* anything.

Hoping he'd never feel *that* way, Sheridan opened his door; but it seemed inevitable that he would; as inevitable, for example, as calling Antonia and telling her to prepare his bill; as inevitable as searching his wallet and discovering he had not sufficient funds to leave the island whether he wanted to do so or not.

Pushing his valise off the table, he leaped over the spilled garments and fell to the floor, where, with his hands pressed over his mouth, he lay smothering back a desire to scream.

Gradually, however, and as he watched it out of the corner of his eye, the bed superseded Rome as an objective. It appeared to be quite as far away as Rome, but much the nicer place to get to. Also, just as he had known his shirts were not really heavy, or the air in the room any heavier than it had been yesterday afternoon, he fully realized the bed was only a few feet away. He could touch it, he wagered; and he did. He approached it slowly on his knees and got in.

Shielded deliciously by blanket and sheet, he followed the sunlight's sentimental arabesques across the tiles and up the papered wall through the shutters, which he had closed. Had there ever been so much time to do nothing in? Sundays, yes. Sundays as a child. The room, like an American Sunday, seemed to have no place to go to in as, through his parted fingers, Sheridan watched it lengthen.

Closing his fingers to block out the room, whose horizon was moving so rapidly away that it made him dizzy, Sheridan cautiously examined the whirlpooling wrinkles crowning his knuckles, which deepened enticingly down almost to the bones, till he effaced them all in a fist. Anxious to touch some cooling object, he turned to the table beside his bed and rested his hands for a moment on the handcuffs. His fingers closed lovingly around them and he took them up and slipped them on. Pressing his wrists together, he experienced an enormous sensual thrill, then ease, relief, rest, and utter peacefulness and well-being down through his entire body to his toes, which he flexed with pleasure when the lock on the handcuffs snapped shut.

After Antonia had brought his lunch, Sheridan lay

watching it dry up. He had buried his locked hands beneath the covers and had been pleased to ask the servant questions about herself without troubling to listen to her replies. Antonia, her tongue tied up in her homeless emotions, told him things she would repeat over to herself while cleaning a hen, a job she loathed, or hunting their eggs, which she adored doing. She would experience pangs of regret at having said, perhaps, some stupid or rash or too familiar thing.

But it was the moment itself, this lovely moment of questions and answers with Signor Sherry, that she would cherish. Smiling, he asked, "Will there be a letter, Antonia?" Antonia, replying in a voice as low as her desire to please was loud, whispered, "Oh yes, today there will be a letter." Leaving him, she closed the doors to his room as tenderly as if they'd been the eyelids of a beloved doll.

The grease had coagulated around the potatoes, the thin slices of veal had grown truffled edges, when Mrs. Markham knocked and came in. She was wearing the simplest white silk shirt and gabardine skirt with a saffron-colored scarf from Capri tied about her waist. Yet when she approached the bed she seemed to Sheridan a creature from the operatic stage. She seemed to be wearing many things of many colors which billowed and shrieked silkenly, then grew still when she did—beside the bed.

The Macaroni

"I think it's outrageous I haven't been told till now," she said. Since knowing Sheridan, and the others, Mrs. Markham had begun to speak of "the town." "The whole town knows but me—or did!"

"Knows? You mean about my condition, Mrs. Markham?"

"Don't be silly, Sheridan. What *has* happened to you?"

"What *could* happen to me?"

"All right. Yes, what—since last night—could have happened to you?" She looked at the cold, ugly food beside him: "Is it because you can't eat it?"

"I think, Mrs. Markham, I've decided just not to. . . ." The steel, or silver, or whatever it was the handcuffs were made of, was warm and sticky now against his flesh. Cooper, he recalled, used to say they were silver; but then Cooper would. Chained to the handcuffs was a tiny key, which it secretly amused Sheridan, at present, to think of Mrs. Markham using to unlock him.

"There is something unreal and wayward about you lying there," she said, gazing thoughtfully into his eyes. "Also, there is something untrue about it. I suggest you get up immediately."

"For God's sake, Mrs. Markham, of course I'm getting up! Didn't you ever stay in bed till two?"

"Till two never. Here, I once stayed in bed till lunchtime; indeed, till you—remember the day?—you yourself roused me." She stepped back swiftly as though to meet a surer, more exacting part of herself. "If we cannot find power within ourselves to help us, then someone else should—help you, I mean, Sheridan. I would not like to see anything unpleasant happen to you."

"That's nice of you, Mrs. Markham," he replied, touched; "but I'm afraid nothing will."

"No, it isn't nice of me. It's more selfish than you know, than you could believe."

"Are you trying to frighten me, Mrs. Markham?"

"I frighten myself," Mrs. Markham replied cautiously. "What I would say if my hands were not, in a sense, tied would seem odd to you, odd and ridiculous to the world—and perhaps wicked——That young man," she said, breaking off from what she'd been saying, "the one who was visiting with you last night, has asked me to go see something with him."

"Is he staying here?" Sheridan asked.

"Yes, I'm sure. At any rate I must tell him it would be impossible for me to go now."

Disregarding Sheridan's protest, Mrs. Markham went to search for Crystal. She was met on the stairs by Antonia carrying a letter. "If that's for Sheridan," she said, and she stopped one step above the servant and held out her hand.

The Macaroni

"I said, if that's for Sheridan, Antonia, I'll take it to him. Is it?" Antonia, placing the letter reluctantly into Mrs. Markham's hand, said it was. "Yes, I thought it was," said Mrs. Markham. She turned and made her way back upstairs. Pausing before Sheridan's doors, she opened her handbag, and before she knew quite what she was doing, slipped the letter in. She entered the room with so low an opinion of herself that she wondered it did not show on her face.

"Ah, I thought it was Antonia," said Sheridan, showing plainly his disappointment.

"No, it's me," Mrs. Markham replied, as though she were ashamed of the fact. She seemed strangely nervous to him.

"Did you? No, you didn't have anything to forget, did you?" Christ, how she bored him!

"I wondered if you needed anything. Cigarettes?"

"No, I don't need a thing. There!" he cried, relieved. "That's Antonia. Will you let her in, please?"

Mrs. Markham opened the door a crack. "Goodness, Antonia, what can you want at this hour of the day? Yes, all right, the tray."

"Yes, Signora Markham," the child said, coming into the room, "the tray."

"No letter, Antonia?"

"Why, yes, Signor Sherry."

"No!" Sheridan cried impatiently, "I mean a letter to-day."

Antonia turned and stared at Mrs. Markham.

"For me, for me," Sheridan cried. "Not for Mrs. Markham, Antonia." Loathing the handcuffs, he dug them into his flesh, shouting as he did so, *A letter for me, idiot!*

"The child is impossible," said Mrs. Markham.

"Signor Sherry," Antonia said, turning slowly from Mrs. Markham to Sheridan, "I will always bring you your letters. Always," she repeated in a hushed, horrified voice, *"always."*

"My God! Why should she be hurt, Mrs. Markham? Why?" Sheridan cried, and, forgetting what he wore, he drew his hands from beneath the covers and thrust them toward the child. Then, "Will one of you get these damned things off me?"

Mrs. Markham felt ill. She felt her breakfast tea and toast had been given one cruel whirl in her stomach. She felt she had turned ludicrously pale at the thought that whatever space there had been between herself and Sheridan had now not only widened but had filled up with laughter!

How depraved! How passive! How ridiculous!

Stilted laughter rocked the room for her, or, rather, hid

the room for her as ticker tape would have done, or balloons. Turning fiercely on Antonia, she directed the child to leave the room and waited till she did. Then, taking the little key exquisitely chained to the handcuffs gently in her fingers, she raised bewildered eyes to Sheridan's brown, attentive ones and, smiling, shook her head as though she could not at all make him out.

"Come, Mrs. Markham," he said, half amused, half impatient with her hesitancy.

"Yes, of course. It's simply that I'm a trifle stunned."

"And I," cried Sheridan, spreading his arms wide, "am free!" He beat his hands together, then fell back in his pillows and, with a sullen air, said, "You've recalled me to life . . . !"

"However painful?"

"Oh, yes," he laughingly replied. "Life, however painful, don't you agree?"

"I do," said Mrs. Markham sternly. "I do indeed!"

[Chapter Seven]

WE ARE IN OUR search for help most circuitous. Mrs. Markham was especially so; for when had she deigned to seek it? When had she ever gone *next door,* or required of a servant more than was prescribed by genteel tradition? It was during Sheridan's subsequent stay in bed that Mrs. Markham became known with a difference to the islanders. Cigarettes for him she obtained from the distrustful-fingered couple who ran the *tabacchi;* fruit, from the young rogue whose shop fronted the piazza; and from Antonia, flowers.

To these people, and to others, Mrs. Markham had

changed from a tourist who had nothing to do, to someone like themselves, they fancied, who had more to do than a little. She was as purposeful to them as their own mothers. Yet how alone she did look!

One bright, hot morning after failing to procure oranges for Sheridan from the rogue, Mrs. Markham left his shop and went searching the piazza for another. As she passed the café owned by the three sisters, the eldest of them, parting the bead curtains, emerged and waved her down.

"I am concerned about Signor Sherry," she said.

Mrs. Markham raised her brows and replied that her own knowledge of Italian was scarce.

"I can be simple, Signora."

I'll bet you can, thought Mrs. Markham, who saw in a sickening flash that her situation with Sheridan, which she considered deep and dark as a well, would be no deeper, nor darker, to this woman than a wine barrel untopped in the sun.

Mrs. Markham knew she needed to be direct with Sheridan; and to be warm without being soft. She needed help with him, and here it was—hatefully close, in the form of a woman with the face of an owl. Mrs. Markham hated her.

"Is Sheridan in debt to you?" she unkindly inquired.

"Certainly. But how is he?"

The Macaroni

"He is resting now," said Mrs. Markham, choosing the very words that least described Sheridan's condition to her. For resting, she felt, was just what he should not be doing. "How much does he owe you, please?"

"Resting? Then has he been so ill? The others have said nothing to me."

"They have said nothing because there is almost nothing to say," explained Mrs. Markham, who had appreciated their staying away from the *pensione* at first, but now questioned their right to do so.

Wary lest she unburden herself to this strange and powerful woman—for she had never let so much of herself unwind as in the past week—Mrs. Markham, to change the subject, asked where she might purchase some oranges.

The eldest sister went and got her some from the café.

"And do you," Mrs. Markham asked, taking them from her, "have any idea what his bill is with you?"

"Tell Signor Sherry not of my concern for his health, Signora, but of my wish to resume our friendship. It is a few hundred lira, the bill."

They both of them stood in the hot sunlight, a thing the Italian would never have done had not Mrs. Markham shown signs of being fairly impossible to guide along common-sense lines into the shade of the trees nearby. Mrs. Markham struck the eldest sister as a childless woman;

while she herself was packed by Mrs. Markham far back and down into the anonymous crowd of females who have so many that they don't know what to do. But Mrs. Markham was wrong, as she frequently was when her feelings were most concerned. They were both childless, except that the larger woman had always been so.

"There, three hundred lira. And the oranges . . . ?"

The eldest sister gave an exasperated pull to the neck of her dress. "Must you pay for them too?"

"I would like to, but . . . ! Well, good-by. I will tell Sheridan you asked for him."

If those who cared enough to remark the change in the American had seen her come into Sheridan's room with the oranges, they would have wondered no longer why she looked lonely.

Consciously assuming the anonymity of a not very bright nurse, Mrs. Markham fussed about the shuttered room making work for herself, for all that really needed doing had been done by Antonia.

She had placed the oranges on the bedside table as though it was a perfectly natural thing to do—which it was not. It was not natural to come into a strange room with oranges, and put them down without remarking the fact. Sheridan waited until she mentioned them.

The Macaroni

"What shall we read, Sheridan?—You know, those oranges were almost amusingly difficult to get!—I've brought a new one today," she said, meaning her book, which, when she held it up, let sprinkle from its middle some seven or eight of its pages.

"Pages, Mrs. Markham? Is that the way for an old schoolteacher to treat a book?" For he had begun a little to hate her, and this was odd in that he liked her. He liked her especially when she read to him, as she was now preparing to do.

"It's all I have," she said, "The *Iliad*. Have you never read it?"

They had gotten through *On the Eve,* and *Fathers and Sons.* She had awakened him one evening after he had fallen asleep so that he might properly hear the ending of *Fathers and Sons.*

She read extremely well and knew it; her voice could rise and fall far beyond the limits it ordinarily did. Once, the first time it had changed to suit a character, Sheridan had actually applauded her efforts. Pleased, Mrs. Markham had looked up from the story.

"That isn't the first time I've heard you applaud, Sheridan; though it is the first you've given me, isn't it?"

She had obviously *lived* a good deal in books, for she took unfeigned pleasure in reading to him, and would sometimes go on reading aloud to herself after Sheridan had fallen asleep.

He was now familiar with the way she held a book while reading about a person she liked, as compared to the manner she held it when the person was not to her taste. For example, in reading the portrait of Paul, in *Fathers and Sons,* she had snatched at the pages of the book, her hands trembling. But tenderly had she read of Bazarov's death. It was after she had awakened Sheridan so that he might hear it. She had been strangely urgent, yet abstract; for her mind had been far more on the story than on her need that Sheridan should hear it. It was another instance of Mrs. Markham coming out of herself, of her unwinding.

They were not three pages into the new book before Sheridan was asleep. The truth was that he'd exhausted himself waiting for Mrs. Markham to come back from town. Glancing up from the book, her eyes took in not only his face, over which a squadron of flies hovered tropically, but also the oranges, which he had refused. She continued to read, but the thought of the oranges occurred ever more strongly to her and made her despair.

They would be there tonight, she thought. They will be there rotting tomorrow as, perhaps, all my gifts to him are bound to do, simply because he does not want gifts, actually, but help. —She knew that what she was reading was making no sense. She was reading aloud the way one walks when exhausted, on and on, unfeelingly.

She closed the book and stared at the flies.

Morbid as was Sheridan's almost infantile claim to excessive sleep, it was not this that primarily depressed, then frightened Mrs. Markham. What did depress her during these silences, which she tried and failed to break by reading aloud to herself, *was* precisely herself.

Self-branded with shame that she could have stooped so low to do so little, she combed her past for a crime wherein her taste—for it was *taste* she thought of—had not been so shockingly in abeyance, if not dead, as it certainly must have been the afternoon when, with scarcely a thought, she had slipped into her purse the letter meant for Sheridan. What she came across in these nervous backward glances at her own life amounted to no more than pictures—charmingly true to memory, but quite untrue to life.

She remembered a child in a pinafore committing uninspirational little thefts of candy that no one ever missed, or of trinkets that soon bored her whether they were missed or not. Her most memorable misdemeanor, perhaps, had been once to wedge a bristling object into the piano in order that she should not have to practice.

Valentine-light as this sort of thing was, Mrs. Markham could find none heavier to weigh up against what she had done to Sheridan. What might have weighed, had she chosen to count it, was her theft of Jonathan—taking him from Markham as though he were *all* hers.

Aware though she was that her subsequent rearing of Jonathan was not as sufficiently unquestionable as she would have liked it to have been, Mrs. Markham never could have been brought to believe she had been wrong about the boy in the beginning. For it was the beginning she remembered, when, pregnant with Jonathan, her blood had coursed so sweetly acquiescent through her veins that every word she heard, and every sound, was "yes." None else had mattered; none was as new. There had been suddenly no noise. It was enough bliss for a lifetime, that beginning. It was all she'd had till now.

She was human, and so wanted what was nearest.

She had been too near the letter not to take it, and she was too near Sheridan not to wonder if her theft was worth it. Once she would have judged her unscrupulousness inevitable and necessary; but because those tactics had lost her Jonathan, Mrs. Markham warned herself to be careful lest she lose what she wanted most because of a letter she had not even thought to open.

She had slipped it into her table drawer, then tried to forget it. Her curiosity, which was never high, was contented with knowing it was from Cooper, and her desire so perversely satisfied with having it that she asked no more from the letter than that it should stay put—and that by staying, it would tend to wear down her guilt, and give all room, all space to her pleasure in possessing.

So keeping the letter without planning to do so, no more, indeed, than she'd planned her theft, Mrs. Markham decided to call on what she now thought of as the awful-rest-of-them: Sheridan's friends. In so doing she spread her own guilt out to a more acceptable thinness. For, she reasoned, if I am guilty of a petty theft, then they, Haller with his so-called Macaroni, are guilty in the betrayal of a specific social duty. They had not, as far as she knew, paid Sheridan a single visit.

About this Mrs. Markham was wonderfully strict. She had to be. She had always to be strict with someone about something. And now, because she could not afford to be severe with herself, and had not really been so with anyone for a long time, she was more than glad to have found somebody new.

This being her first release since the handcuff incident, which had so oppressed her that she dared not think of it except as having happened to someone she barely knew, Mrs. Markham, in rising, and in putting down her book, did both things a shade vehemently. Before stepping into the hall, she glanced back at Sheridan. His eyes closed.

Friends and Vague Lovers

"Did you want something, Sheridan?"

She knew as she spoke that he would not reply, would not admit that he'd been awake watching her. Not even his sleep is real, she thought.

For an instant Mrs. Markham felt she was in a world dominated by halves; the world itself seemed but half a world in half-light lighting just one side of everybody, and that side their weakest and worst.

The house which Haller shared with Billy Helion was the last one on the street. It was not unlike what used to be known in America as a carriage house. Its green doors were high and wide enough for a carriage or car to pass between them. Alongside these doors grew a vine of wisteria which climbed the front of the house and all but hid a tiny balcony. To the right of the balcony was an open window at which Haller sat absorbed in his work. On the sunny sill sprawled his cat, blindly licking its ball of a paw.

Mrs. Markham needed help with Sheridan, but she did not like it that she did: she waited till Haller looked down at her. "Will I disturb you?" she asked. "Do you remember me? We talked once together at your party—rather, I talked with Mr. Helion. Is *he* in?"

It was typical of Mrs. Markham not to have noticed the wisteria till she inhaled its perfume. Pulling off a sprig, she carried it intently to her nose as she went up.

The Macaroni

"But it was about your paintings," she said, coming into the room, "your painting, that is, that we talked about, and not you."

She did not look at the painting because of the cat. The cat rather annoyed her; it seemed to have known before she did exactly where she had planned to sit. Haller called it to him.

"I hope," he said, "you haven't had trouble finding us."

Mrs. Markham shook her head impatiently.

"I have the feeling you've been expecting me," she said —too carelessly.

"Expecting you? No."

"To call, I mean?"

"No."

She glanced down at her lap, then quickly up into Haller's eyes, as though, in that instant, she had invited him, by looking away, to shift his position to a more vulnerable one: the thought that he might not be wearing his artificial leg gave her an odd and somewhat necessary feeling of superiority.

"I've come about Sheridan," she said abruptly. "I think it's outrageous that not one of you have visited him."

Gazing steadily at her, Haller stooped and scooped up the cat. Between them settled a spell of silence. Then: "*Your* son killed himself, didn't he?"

They both sat moved and wretched. Haller had been

working; he saw no reason to have been interrupted by an idle woman whose long, thin face recalled Boston to him in the form of an early tombstone. Mrs. Markham, who had not expected brutality, was no readier for it than she'd ever been. Reaching miles up for the neck of her dress, she found a solitary mother-of-pearl button: she had once heard that by holding to something frail as a button, a piece of string, you can successfully combat the feeling you have that you are about to fall.

Faintly she murmured, "You are even more serious than I thought. I dread the pride of serious people."

Turning the button round and round on its thread, she sank into the corner of the couch and closed her eyes. "Don't accuse me, please," she said, and there flitted across her face the veil of a smile. "Why, Jonathan was my hour. We none of us have more than that, do we? And so he was mine. How far back you make it seem. . . ."

Searching out her handkerchief, she held it for a moment against her eyes. "You were wrong," she murmured admonishingly, "to say that."

Evasively Haller replied that she was right. "Still, you should know about him, shouldn't you? Isn't that why you've come here?"

Mrs. Markham didn't know. She listened to the silence; a hush seemed to have come in with her from the bright, still street. We need a third here, she thought, and she realized how necessary Helion must be to Haller. Haller's pale, intense face, with its unchanging, immobile smile, his full, pale lips pledged, it seemed to her, to impossible purity, made Mrs. Markham feel close and unfriendly to him. She remembered his loss of a limb again, and saw in his protestant strength and weakness a reflection of her own strength, which was her weakness.

"I don't know that I should know any more than I do now about Sheridan."

"I do," said Haller. "I think you should know that he probably hates you." He covered the cat's head with his hand; its ears slipped up between his fingers like arrowheads. "I first began to avoid Sheridan in the army. It was in the army, you see, that we met. He seemed to have put all his nerves away, and to be living in a sort of incomplete sleep. Sherry needs always many ways out of whatever situation he happens to be in; it's as though he'd been taught that is the only way to live. In the infantry there are just two ways out—to go crazy, or to die. One may get out with a wound, but if it's a real wound one never gets over it. Our eventual devotion to each other followed pretty closely along army lines, except that it was necessarily oblique. I did not claim anything from him, but Sheridan wanted a great deal from me.

"In German forests the thought that he might get wounded and not killed used to wake me. The wound, if it ever happened, would have been a ghastly one, unfair to him as his getting killed, say, could not be. I mentioned this to him once. He frowned and told me not to worry so about myself.

"Since the war he's lived with Cooper, who has supported him with money, but not, I don't think, with much more. All that comes from *his* side. I'm sure Cooper's the first person he's ever left. It's an awful thing to see people do what they're not used to doing: they do it so embarrassingly."

Mrs. Markham thought so too. She thought it all such a letdown. Haller was right. Why do people devil themselves into believing they can change? Why hadn't Sheridan remained as he was when she'd first seen him? She warned herself, however, that Sheridan *was* the young man back at the Pensione Morabido. He was; but she did not approve. He had no pride! But then, when had he ever? How could he have had it, avoiding, as he had, facing up all these years to obtaining—well, his bread?

Remembering that his bread was exactly what Sheridan had gotten, Mrs. Markham, fairly begging for information that would enable her to forgive as well as forget, asked, "Isn't there something about his being an orphan?"

"Oh God yes!" Haller laughingly replied. "Sherry's a grand orphan!"

The Macaroni

"Grand?"

"Grandly persistent. He was not the orphan to dive overboard to retrieve the parasol, or handbag, or whatever it was the millionaire's little daughter let fall into Horatio Alger's Hudson. He would have stood still, beautifully still, and let whatever diving there was to be done up to the millionaire. But there was never to be a millionaire. He was befriended at a necessarily early age by a church organist who wore a wig and had a little house off Christopher Street in New York. Sherry once pointed it out to me.

"It was a year or so after the war. He was dressed extremely well, and was due to go off to Europe with Cooper. We stood, the two of us, by a little grill fencing the house, and Sheridan pointed down through it at the basement windows. 'I lived there once, Haller,' he said to me. Then he did something charming, strange. He took some ticket stubs from his coat pocket—he has a habit of keeping things like that—tore them very carefully into bits, and sprinkled them down over the grime and dust that no one, apparently, ever bothered to clean away any more. He stood looking for a minute at the steps and window sills—then he burst out laughing! He explained how he'd found the old boy dead one morning with his wig inside out over his face.

"I was rather fascinated with the house where Sherry had been, after a fashion, raised. But it had been turned into a rooming house, and looked tired enough to fall down; it gave off very little of the old organist, who, it seems, used to collect pictures, too.

"Then there were others. One rather notorious man called Farrell who, it seems, put Sherry into a fashionable school for awhile for fun. They were in a motor accident. Farrell came out of it looking piously toward marriage and a family: you see, Sherry's terribly used to being let down. As far as I know his leavetaking of Cooper, if it is *just* of Cooper, has set a precedent."

"I suppose," said Mrs. Markham, in a faint, unenthusiastic voice, "that he's always *looked* promising."

Haller's reaction to this showed her she'd been appreciated for the first time. She did not know there would be a second time, and scarcely cared. But for the moment she indulged her tiredness in the agreeable sensation of being involved in a conspiracy innocent as it was tender—for she had meant what she said tenderly. "But don't you feel," she asked, "that he's been more taken from than given to?" Haller shrugged his shoulders. "I do," Mrs. Markham cried. "I know he has."

"And you," Haller questioned her, "have you taken from him?"

"Oh yes," Mrs. Markham replied, "as much as ever I could."

"Too much?"

"To keep, yes. It's strange the feelings I have. . . ."

"How, strange?"

"Well, like a thief's."

"And, then, is this why you've come here today?"

"I have no idea," she said, rising and going slowly to him. "No, no idea at all."

Haller considered she was really quite beyond being hurt, though not beyond a certain pity. However, he was grateful to her for not overworking her courage with him as he rather suspected she would have done had she liked him. He stood up for the first time, and they shook hands and parted.

An hour later Haller slipped into Sheridan's room unannounced.

[*Chapter Eight*]

THERE WAS a murmur of voices, a green dissembling light, an odor of roses and orange. Slats of thin sun cut across a corner of the bed, whose occupants appeared as remote to Haller, for an instant, as stone flowers in a paper-weight of glass. Sheridan sat pasha fashion in a chamois vest and shorts, slowly lifting spoons of rice to his mouth. The rest, Mrs. Christophe, Billy Helion, and John Harness, looked out at Haller as from an unspecific jail.

A host of memories came to him of Baltimore summers, where, with a newspaper between his body and the rug, he had as a boy slept away such hot afternoons as this. Outside, beyond the painted window screens, was the green, hot hedge, the slow, steady fermentation of rootbeer set in bottles on the lawn. There had been a bowl of roses, just such a smell of orange.

"Hallelujah darling!" exclaimed Mrs. Christophe. "How did you know . . . ?"

"The roses, Chris—" He bent and kissed her, not as though she had just broken a moment for him, but as though she had made one. "The roses you brought, brought me."

"You know, they'll never do that play," said John Harness, somewhat mysteriously.

"Oh, I'm sure they will, my dear," Mrs. Christophe told him with a sad, trancelike smile. "Just you stay away from them long enough and they'll do it."

"*Red Roses For Me,* I mean."

"I know, I know." She patted his knee. "Just do as I say, and stay away."

Theirs was a *fête champêtre* somewhat confused in time and place. History seemed to have met here and had an accident. John Harness, for instance, was the square-jawed crusader come home hunting the innocence he had lost in the Holy Land. Squired by Billy, domestic as an egg, John's nostrils flared widely indignant at Billy's bumpkin, "We're having a picnic, Haller."

The Macaroni

"What a sordid idea! Imagine a picnic in bed."

"As children," Billy pursued wistfully, "most of us adored eating in bed. I used to dream of a crowded bed, all of us poor and loving."

"And I," said Mrs. Christophe, "dreamed of a bed of my own. We slept three in one when I was a kid, two at the top, one at the bottom."

"It sounds like heaven."

Mrs. Christophe wasn't sure. "Even then, you see, I was a go-getter. I guess what I wanted was a white bed pure as a cake of soap. And sometimes," she added, bitterly, "I think that's just what I did get."

Into her bluejeans, which she wore with a rather competitive air, Mrs. Christophe had stuffed the ends of an old-fashioned lace blouse. Her hair was unusually quiet. "I've cut it," she explained, looking up at Haller like a Renoir that had run.

"So how was Arezzo, Chris?"

"Arezzo? Ah yes, Piero. *The* Pieros, as Chris would say."

"Piero della Francesca's 'Resurrection' is at Arezzo then?" said John Harness. Bending toward Mrs. Christophe, he covered the back of her hand with his own. "I must see it. Perhaps we can go together. You see, a friend of mine had a wonderful idea of blowing up a photograph of it as a background for *Crime and Punishment.* What do you think of that, Mrs. Christophe? Blowing it up, I mean?"

"Divine. But it isn't at Arezzo, darling. It's— Do you have a cigarette?"

"I did. I had a whole pack of Chesterfields when I came in."

Mrs. Christophe took an Italian one from Haller.

"We never went," she said. "We're still here—all of us."

"Then what finally happened to the aeronautics student?"

"Stop!" Mrs. Christophe cried, stopping her ears and making a terrible face. "I know only too well where he is. He's where we are, wherever we are. Night after night, through meal on meal, Chris and he sit discussing the Lake poets while I sing folk songs to myself, or sweet nothings, as the case may be. Anyway, it's all horribly *rural!*"

"I knew he was a pig! Only a nasty little opportunistic pig could have managed to cadge enough drinks to get drunk on at a party like ours was."

"Cage, by the way, is his name, Billy. Leslie Cage. Oh, and that motorcycle!" Mrs. Christophe shuddered. "You know, I mind it for him while he goes into saloons and things."

"And you," Haller asked, crossing the room, "do you ride?"

Mrs. Christophe watched him with sullen eyes when he opened the shutters and went out on the balcony. "They ride me when they feel like it," she said to the others. "You see, my dears, that's why I'm here today. I couldn't stand being left with a motorcycle through a *festa*. I've come to get you all to go." She held her glass out to Sheridan as though it were a mouth asking to be kissed. He brought up the wine bottle from the floor and poured her some. "Tell us about Leslie Cage," he said, smiling.

Doggishly grateful for his attention, Mrs. Christophe sipped her wine and giggled. Then, with what warmth or courage she took from it, she regained something of her boisterous self, that self that compelled her to sing for her supper even when she knew there would be none.

"Well," she said, slapping her bluejeans, "he wears these things, naturally, and a sweater with a little white bib of a T-shirt. Whenever I see him he looks as if he's going to say '*Gee!*' and the hell of it is he usually does."

There was the roar of a motorcycle from the street, which stopped just long enough for Haller to think he could be heard when he turned and said something into the room. Mrs. Christophe rose straight up from the bed, the wine in her glass hardly stirring. Going to the door, she reached for the knob with the hand that still held the glass. "Did you see what I——!" She put the glass down on the floor, and wiped the back of her hand on her bluejeans. "Now don't forget me tonight, dolls. Sherry, do you hear? Haller?" Haller was still on the balcony, his back to her. She waved good-by to him and to the others a minute later from the

[137]

street, but they were not seeing her. Shading their eyes, they gazed over the tops of the houses at the beach.

Out by the sea wall Crystal was kicking a ball around with some Italian boys. The scene had a faraway air of intensity about it in that none of the players uttered a sound. All you heard from the balcony was the thud of the ball against naked feet, or the muted sound of it against heads. The ball came constantly at Crystal, who, having failed miserably in his attempts to stop it with his head as the Italians did, was now simply using his feet. Stopping the ball with his knee, he sent it into the sea and turned his back on it and on the boys, all of whom broke into the wildest laughter. Fetching the ball, one boy punted it heavily back across the sand at Crystal. This time he kicked it far into the sea. The boys surrounded him, and again the scene was silent, intense.

"Where is the United States Cavalry? Thank God!" Billy Helion shouted, and he and Harness tore out of the *pensione* and made for the beach. They had just rounded the corner of the wharf, when Mrs. Christophe, riding third, tore by on the motorcycle.

"Poor darling," Sheridan said, looking after her, "I'll bet she's known more Leslies than she can count."

"No, she counts very well," Haller replied, smiling. "It's the *gamin* act that's got you, Sherry, and I can see why. Her other act is so awful it doesn't leave you any choice but to like her this way. But I wouldn't worry about her any more than she worries about the Leslies she and Chris have left behind them. She's nuts about him, as you know, and equally nuts about furthering both their careers. I forget with her that there's anything *but* career."

"Somehow," said Sheridan, "I think there's always been more. I feel her life with Chris calls out a very secret angel in her."

"I'm not an authority on the angel, Sherry; but of skeletons now"— he bowed at the next balcony. "Speaking of which, there's your gaunt ladybird friend." He bowed again.

Mrs. Markham, who had come out on her balcony, had not seen them, or was pretending not to; her attention was being given to Crystal, who, by now, was swimming toward the ball he had kicked into the sea. A few of the Italian boys lined the shore cheering him on, but most of them, made self-conscious by the presence of Billy Helion and John, had retired to mope in the shade of a fishing boat.

Haller turned to his friend with the concentrated air of a person absorbed in a puzzle. "Tell me, Sherry," he asked in a voice meant to be overheard, "is it true that you're afraid you won't be wanted if you go back to Cooper?"

"It wouldn't," Sheridan replied uneasily, "be the first time, would it?—Shall we go in?"

"No, but it would be *another* time, wouldn't it, Sherry?"

"Really, Haller, how lousy you are at talking practically: you don't know how to do it, you know."

"*Am* I being practical?"

"No, but you are being goddamned rude. Will you, for Christ's sake, come in here."

"In that case," said Haller, pursuing him into the room, "I'll be what you call ruder still, and offer to pay your passage home."

"Home?—Are you crazy?"

A confused, hurt, then blank look—each routing the other—came over Sheridan's face. His body, which had tensed at the word "home," gradually and contritely bent in all its visible joints, the knees, the elbows, the neck. What was frightened in him rushed to hiding behind a just perceptible puffiness, which for an instant showed everywhere on his face, but notably about the mouth.

"It would be like you, Haller," he said in a voice low and pitchless, "to do—something——"

The rest of what he had to say got caught in a choke. Thrusting his fist to his mouth, he stood as though retching into it. A derisive shout of applause broke into the room from the beach. Sheridan raised his head smiling the way men do who have been struck in the face by a woman. Avoiding each other's eyes, both he and Haller went out on the balcony.

The Macaroni

Crystal stood at the edge of the water holding the wet ball. He might have been smiling. The outlines of his short, tight body appeared to be greatly exhilarated. Suddenly the Italian boys rushed him and whisked him up running on their shoulders like a little brown god holding the world. Cutting the water's edge with their brown leathery shins they ran to the stone steps leading to the sea wall. Halfway up the steps, the boys put Crystal down. Then one by one they trotted out to the end of the wall and dived into the sea out of sight.

"We were talking about—money, weren't we, Sherry?"

"Yes. Well, there's no need, really. Cooper has sent me some, or says he has. I don't understand actually, because according to him it's been two weeks coming. Now he's saying I got it, and that I'm a liar, and so on. You see, he insists on my playing games to amuse him still."

"So do most of us, I'm afraid. By the way, who does bring you your mail? Markham . . . ?"

Following the direction of Haller's glance, Sheridan turned to look for his neighbor, but she had gone. "She's brought one or two, yes. You mean, of course, that she's kept all the others?"

"I don't at all. Just one would give her far more trouble than she'd think it was worth. You see, we are very alike, your friend and I, Sherry. We're both somewhat burnt out.

It's what's left of our separate wishes we once had—! Well, to die."

"And—do you still?"

"Oh no. *That* could hardly have lasted long. What we experienced was a sense of loss. Hers, I suspect, was very great." He paused and watched the Italian boys and Crystal gather up their clothes from the dark sand. Helion and John Harness sat on the sea wall respectfully awaiting sunset. "What we know," Haller continued, "makes us unbearable to each other. We're only able to accept the Billies and Harnesses and Christophes because what we want from people is a sense of life however small—and it is, of necessity, always small. When it's big, it's too big. You know about the giant Cyclops, Ulysses had to blind in order to escape? Well, memory is our Cyclops that time has almost helped us blind—time, and Billy, and darlings like you."

"But what's this got to do . . . ?"

"Everything: she wants you as you were."

"And you? Do you, Haller?"

"Didn't I say we were alike? Of course I do."

Sheridan shrugged his shoulders and went in and got into bed. "I must say, you've made a very large study of Mrs. Markham on nothing."

"That's stupid of you."

"And typical of you, Haller."

The Macaroni

Haller raised his arm to Billy and Harness, who were now walking slowly his way across the beach. Both raised their arms to him. "I'm going now, Sherry," he said, coming into the room. "She came to see me today," he confessed. "She said something that at the time I thought was sheer corn. Then, for no reason at all, she got up and left. What she said was that she'd taken something from you, and that she felt like a thief." He moved toward the door, saying, "I guess there's no point in asking you to come along tonight, is there?"

"No point, you bastard——"

"No—but if I've talked against her, I've talked against myself too. We are, after all, the people who matter. One cannot know life without knowing what we do."

Shielded by Mrs. Markham's copy of the *Iliad,* Sheridan leaped from his bed as soon as Haller left, and peeped over his balcony. What had Haller told her? What, thinking aloud in his innocence, had Haller then said? Or was it what Mrs. Markham had said to Haller? Couldn't he just see them, though, making an image of him and kindly bleeding it to death with pins. What, after all, was real to either of them but some dreadful piece of their pasts they both pretended to be resigned to? How did they know what they pretended to know about themselves? Who were they to assume they knew to the minute which day was good, which bad, and exactly when the moment was that broke them?

His own past lay half concealed on the surface of his mind, a lumpy surface, rather, which when he attempted to view it stretched suddenly taut, and bounced down days into eternity with an air of packages that had never been opened.

Sheridan's gaze spilled over the pages of the *Iliad* and picked with possessive interest at the crowds passing out of town to the *festa* five miles away. Orphans appareled in blue parted swimmingly to let a truck by—itself chucked with families rigid as Easter plants. Mrs. Markham, he expected, would not be able: "I will not be able"—couldn't he just hear her—"to read to you tonight, Sheridan; because, you see, there's this *festa*; something one should see, I suppose; though I . . ."

Big-throated bands of *contadini* streamed beneath his thoughts; darkness fell around the forms of horses; carriage lamps pointed a smoky-gold line out of town.

Leaning his head back against the balcony door, Sheridan casually crossed his legs when he heard Mrs. Markham open her door. He did not move when the door closed, or when he heard her footsteps in the hall; but to the sound of her voice he stiffened. Expectancy made him thinner: his stomach left the touching line of his shorts. The hairs on his chest rose, or seemed to; and when he raised the book there, they scraped wirelike at the pages, making a tiny, wiry, boxed-in sound.

Answering whatever Mrs. Markham had said, there came a reply from Crystal, the desperate camaraderie of their steps on the stair. No, he thought, she was not even to say she would not be able. But if the expected had made him thin, the unexpected filled him, typically, with self-pity: for an instant he wondered if he was to weep.

She stood below wearing a combination of two suits; a thing she had not, to Sheridan's knowledge, done before. Pearls weighted the lobes of her ears. Crystal, beside her, talked a blue streak, in answer to which she appeared to be saying nothing, only raising her arm, putting out her hand from time to time as though to restrain him.

No, thought Sheridan, she does not like him.

That he should care whether she did or not made him feel he needed to laugh. Actually he wept with very real pleasure for as long as it took Mrs. Markham's escort to procure a carriage. It creaked like seven doors when they got into it, and spread backwards like an accordion when they sat down. Its horse, an old pale thing, did not move till he was whipped.

Mrs. Markham and Crystal looked as vulnerable as chil-

dren on their way to a wake. He could not despise them
though he tried. Their innocence, their inability to be anything, suddenly, but cripplingly sensitive, did not allow
them to lounge back in their seats. Accusingly straight-
backed they sat going to their mother's funeral; and, naturally, they would laugh, and someone would crack them
on their heads with knuckles stretched blue. Then they
would feel *they* had killed her. . . . All this took them out
of sight; the poor old horse, the little dim lamps dimmer
than all the others, and the two touchingly vulnerable
backs—all were gone now and lost to him in the dark. He
felt dry and weak and refreshed.   •

Antonia had come to clear away the remains of the party.
His supper sat smoking up into the light of the lamp she
had turned on. "Antonia?" he asked, breaking the fantasy
that it was Cooper who had come in and not the servant.
"There is," he told her, "a glass on the floor by the door."
Chris had left it. Dear Chris, she had brought him roses.
Haller he forgave. The memory of his afternoon party en-
closed him like perfume: a picnic in bed, Billy had called
it. How nice they all were, really. How nice, in one sense,
Haller had been to offer the money. Why shouldn't he take
it? No, he couldn't. Cooper's would come, a last lousy,
sentimental check. Then Paris. Or somewhere.

He stopped and thought suddenly that he was standing

here on the balcony choosing places to go to when, actually, he had no choice but to stay where he was until his money arrived. Still and all, he thought, smiling, I am choosing! I do feel at last that I'll get out!

Turning from the room, he began to softly whistle.

The thought of his unpaid bill mounting with every mouthful he took at the *pensione* reached for him when he stepped forward to the edge of the balcony, so that he had to move fast to forget it. For what counted with Sheridan was not what he knew, but what he knew he should forget. Ah forget it, he told himself; and, bending far over the rail, he smiled down into the crowd.

He was ready and smiling should someone smile up at him. He was all ears should someone call his name. For one excited moment opportunity surrounded him, and his eyes, as though turned to rain, poured over every head in the crowd.

Down in the street, seated grandly in her rented carriage, was the eldest sister, handsomely costumed in green. When she spoke up to him he heard not what she said, but only the strength with which she said it; borrowing as much of it as he could, Sheridan told himself he would not go back to Cooper, or to Rome.

[*Chapter Nine*]

"In Italy the poor are everywhere visible, Signor Sherry. Look at the men who work too long and too hard for too little because those who own too much do next to nothing about it. Here the poor have taken the responsibility of their poverty, but the rich with their riches have not."

Thus the eldest sister talked as she moved toward the white and golden altar in the midst of the hotly swaying *festa* crowd. Sheridan had hardly recognized her. For she displayed a taste for finery ·in her attire such as he had thought her to be indifferent to. Her small owlish face was paler than ever. There was a gaslit look about her like a woman in Lautrec.

"I have had my hair dyed," she explained.

"It looks very well, Signora."

"No. It looks foolish; but the act itself was not so, in that it helped me over a small depression."

She gave a downward tug to her dress, and smiled, which she rarely did. "I also bought this."

"It is a beautiful green."

At the altar she knelt and kissed, in her turn, a scepter which the officiating priest then wiped and presented to the lips of another pilgrim.

"It is perhaps too green," the eldest sister said, rising.

Sheridan offered her his arm, and they emerged through a door off the transept into the welcome sea air. Numerous colored lights hung like Christmas balls between the *festa* and the starry sky. A band played selections from *Norma*.

"*However*," the eldest sister continued, "one should not be ashamed for too long of what one does. You either make peace with your actions, or else change them. Do not persist in believing you are one thing"—a tiny whore in cast-off lizard skin shoes divided them—"*and*," the eldest sister cried adamantly, "your actions another. We are only what we do. This is plain to me. I have led a full life—and know. I am also aware that I am talking too much."

The Macaroni

Turning slowly and heavily, though gracefully, on her heel, she gave her attention to a hill by the sea lit to blazing with seven rows of torches.

"When I was very young I was up there with the men amongst those torches looking down on all this. Now I am perhaps too gross to walk between them without catching fire; but the days when I could do so are memorable to me. They do not deserve forgetting."

"You are very brave, Signora."

"*Never!* I never climbed it but I trembled, and the more I trembled, the higher I climbed. Naturally I had not yet reached the age when one knows it is too late to change."

"That is not so late," Sheridan shouted over the noise of a passing truck, "*is it?*"

"No; but it *is* late, whereas all the rest is early."

Families split to let the truck by, then came together minus their old folk, the more enterprising of whom lit off to beg.

Not the least of the *festa's* loud wonders—for the pavilions were doing *nothing*—was Leslie Cage's motorcycle, which he had sympathetically travestied in streamers. On the seat behind Leslie rode Mr. Christophe. "You remember Cage, don't you, Sherry?" he shouted in a play-intermission voice. They stopped and shook hands.

"I'm afraid I was pretty awful at that party," said Cage.

"One drink or two, and I'm out."

Out to get all you can, thought Sheridan, echoing not his own thoughts, actually, but those of others less willing than he himself was to take Cage at face value. Like Mr. Christophe, Cage was notably tall and thin; but against Christophe's professorial sag, the young man looked as if he'd yet to bend over anything more complicated than apple pie.

Mr. Christophe invited Sheridan and the Signora to a pavilion where Chris and Haller were. "We'll meet you there later," he said, but as an afterthought it was acutely lacking the impromptu air he obviously meant it to have.

"*Mrs.* Chris is just raring to go!" said Cage, with apparently no idea that if she was, he was the reason why.

People kept insisting on being startled by the motorcycle. For it coughed and rasped and was held back from flying at them only by the fact, certainly, of its being weighted with two bodies. Finally, after an exhausting period of false starts, the chunky vehicle roared its elongated riders unceremoniously away into the crowd.

"*Which,*" the Signora inquired, "is the married one?" Sheridan told her, but corrected her gently when she commenced to rhapsodize. "My friend's marriage, Signora, is unique, and generally difficult."

"I speak of weddings, Signor. You will not marry; but

The Macaroni

all the rest is nonsense. And a wedding is, as a principle, a good and lasting thing. I had a good, firm, lasting one. I would do it again. My husband was less boring than most men, not the least attractive to other women; but to me, yes. He complemented me in every way, besides being a Northerner—a Roman. But he was an idealist, as I have already informed you, and so was not meant for too long a life.—A perfectionist, and only the dead are perfect, though I have heard of some exploding vilely."

Outside the pavilion designated by Christophe, the eldest sister said, strangely, Sheridan thought, that, no, she would not go in. "Cafés rouse up too much of a sense in me of when I began in one as a girl. If they are worse than mine, they depress me; but more real is the pain I feel if they are superior. It would be most depressing, this one, for it has no roof; and to see money made in a café made of air would pain me."

"If you like I will not go in, Signora."

"The cyclist expects you."

"It is his wife who is my friend."

"Yes, it is natural you should go in."

"And you . . . ?"

"Me . . . ? Good God! I was born here!"

She moved off, bowing from right to left to the people she passed. Then, sweeping around one of the little bazaars she despised, and from which a few wooden dolls fell like courtiers on their faces in the dust, she entered a shop.

To get out on the pavilion Sheridan passed down a latticed archway lined with tables of fish and *pasta,* over which tiny Maypoles of colored paper stood doing nothing to hordes of victorious flies.

The pavilion smelled of the sea, and, indeed, looked out on it. Mrs. Christophe and Haller did not. Belligerent, and drunk in a regiment of silently fluttering empty tables, they were only just barely looking at each other.

Except for a painted seashell necklace, whose colors were coming off on her neck, Mrs. Christophe had not changed any of her *gamin* costume since her afternoon visit to the Pensione Morabido. Haller, who rarely got drunk but he got soaking, wore a dark, vengeful suit. They were nervous and still as overworked dancers. Half-moons of depression hung beneath their eyes.

"What *you* don't understand, Haller, are the things people can't question; things too precious; things that a too close examination might destroy. Candlelight is the most light a lot of—shall we say *relationships?*—can stand. And don't give me that painting line: painting's me; but Chris, awful as you might think it, is the reason I paint, the reason I do this—and the reason I do that!"

"This" was a glass; "that," a cigarette.

The Macaroni

"Painting was for me a way of life that I wanted when I was a kid. It was the way I could get it, I mean, and I did. A damned ambitious kid, I was, too, as you can imagine, stuck in one of a row of frightened little houses in Lambertville."

"She said," said Haller, "wistfully."

"Sherry, you listen to this. This bastard's heard everything. Across the river from Lambertville was New Hope, cozy as a pillow, and as stuffy. Oh, they had lamps, Sherry, and we didn't. They had white houses and Jo Davidson and a great big Victorian cat in the shape of a cloud purring down the back of their stylish pessimism. Whatever they had, I wanted it. But I wasn't for long like the snotty little thing in that Mansfield story who *seed* the lamp. My mother was a tough, straight-backed, rather awful little Quaker of a thing, with elbows the color and texture of chicken feet. She put teeth in my dreams that she'd never quite known how to put into her own. I'll never forget her at my first show in New York. Chris, I guess, had given her a drink; and she sat holding it for hours on her lap with her gloves. People came and went, and there she sat as though she were counting them. I tried not to see her, and she, bless her, tried to help me not to see her. *Her lips kept moving.* I was as hard as she'd wanted me to be; but hard as she was, there was still sweetness enough in her to make me cringe at the strangers we'd become. Whole areas of her were still green and unsatisfied till the day she died.— You've come like a good doll, Sherry. How nice of you."

"Don't cry, baby. . . ."

"No, Haller," she said, drawing her hand away from Sheridan, "I know that I have what I want most, because it's the thing in my life I question least."

"Bravo . . . ?"

"I don't say that you *should* question," said Haller wearily. "I just say that maybe there should be room in every what-you-may-call-it, to allow for the question—and the answer."

Mrs. Christophe replied doggedly, "I know if I asked too hard, or maybe even at all, I'd lose what I have."

"Well, then," Haller shot out, "maybe you should!"

To this, Mrs. Christophe simply stared.

"*Of course* not all of us should ask questions," said Haller, hurt that he had hurt her. "Sherry shouldn't. Why, one little question might . . . Then, goodness! What a pity that would be for all of us. I mean, Sherry, that I don't for a minute think you ought to question your—neighbor?"

"Have you a neighbor, Sherry, darling? I have Leslie. Yours is that American lady who's had a tragedy. Do you like her? I hope so. Don't listen to Haller, my dear; he's just a shell. Yes, that's what you are, Haller, a shell full of horrible old echoes."

The Macaroni

Emotionally, Haller slanted downward. He knew he walked through a conversation like a sniper—to kill it, but he loathed being told he did. It gave him a lonely, cut-off feeling. These two, he mused, are friends. The thought that they could touch each other, and that he could not touch either of them, pained him.

He was glad for Billy when he came; but annoyed, rather, that he was trailed by their not in the least mutual friend, Harness.

"Tying one on, Haller?"

"It's already on, thank you, Billy."

Billy turned his disapproving face on Mrs. Christophe. "Leslie's wearing cowboy boots," he said to her as if it were her fault.

"*He is?*" Mrs. Christophe replied in too high a voice. Then, calling the waiter, she changed to grappa.

"Should you, Mrs. Christophe?" Harness wondered.

"Of course I should, and so should you. *You* should bathe in it! Billy, push these goddamned tables together; and stop looking like somebody slipped a slug down your Upright!"

Billy stood for seconds bristling, but he could no more help doing what he was told to do than he could help getting angry at being told to do it. So with the willing help of John Harness, the tables were put together, during which process not more than one glass was broken.

[157]

Friends and Vague Lovers

For all his timidity, there was a great deal Billy Helion recognized that others, supposedly more gifted, did not. Insisting on continuity in the littlest things, he had always the table set, as it were, for each coming meal, and the fire going beneath the pot, the pot going toward readiness. Behind their house was a garden through which he made watertracks to needy plants. It was Billy's way, Haller had often thought, watching him, of saying his beads: Water to this one, water to that, and water to you when I get to you, which, with the help of God, will be soon.

So naturally he put the tables together; but it was Mrs. Christophe who broke the glass over which Leslie Cage appeared like a genie, all boots and bluejeans and tight T-shirt.

"Pay up, Chris," he said, striding good-naturedly toward her, his thumbs crooked on his belt like a smile.

"Now that motorcycle of yours," Harness, who had not yet met him, began.

"Won't you sit down?" Loudly, from Billy.

"Well, I find it pretty impossible, you see—to sit, I mean, with all this going on."

"All what?" Mrs. Christophe asked up her sleeve. *"All what?"*

Plunging his thumb up into the air with a hitchhiker's gesture, Cage explained, "Why, all this, Mrs. Chris. This lovely *festa.*"

The Macaroni

"Ahh—balls!"

Cage shrugged his shoulders at everybody else. "But thank you, anyway, Billy," he said, and he went toward the arch.

"You better watch those heels, *Mary!*"

"I beg your pardon—ma'am?"

"I said, watch those heels you're wearing, *Spike!*"

"Mrs. Christophe," Cage said, coming back to the table. "I'm sorry for you, you hear? If there's anything I can do for you, I will. I seem to be bothering you more and more."

"Listen to him! Who the hell do you think you are, the Virginian? Move on, Stagecoach, your passenger's showing! —God!" she moaned, striking her forehead, "that I should be subjected to this in my old age."

"*Won't* you sit down!" cried Billy, kicking a chair out from under his table.

"Yes, do," said Harness. "I'd like to know just how much fuel that motorcycle of yours takes. I thought maybe it'd be a good thing to get around in."

"Not much," Cage replied, distracted. "Maybe we can talk about all that later. We will meet—later . . . ?"

"Always willing, Tex," Mrs. Christophe shouted after him when he went out, "just name your weapon; mine's rat poison!"

She buried her head in her arms. "Oh, what a fool am I, huh, Haller? What a fool . . . !"

Friends and Vague Lovers

"It's that grappa, Mrs. Christophe," Harness told her. "Why, I remember once——"

Mrs. Christophe raised her head. "Not once, but always. You're always remembering, and you always have a friend. Do you *really* have so many?"

"What's that, Mrs. Christophe? Friends? Why, yes—don't you?"

"Yes, but I don't like them."

"Like what, Chris?" asked Mr. Christophe, who had been sent in on the run by Cage. He bent tenderly over Mrs. Christophe as though she were a child. Anguish was the flavoring Mrs. Christophe most appreciated in her relationship with Christophe. She could not imagine a marriage that was not *trying*, or one that could be interesting as well as *safe*. Never sure of her husband, it was when she was least sure of him that she loved him most. Their marriage, good above and beyond promise, looked miserable when seen as one necessarily had to see it at present, while it contained an intruder. That the intruder was innocent, which was frequently so because Mr. Christophe preferred it so, meant nothing to Mrs. Christophe. She saw Cage as a devil, and down him she would if it killed her. It was interesting that she had downed as many devils as she most certainly had, for during these skirmishes Mrs. Christophe lay wide open as a harbor.

The Macaroni

"Friends, Chris," she replied without roughness. "We were talking about friends."

Gazing up beyond the electric lights at the stars, Billy Helion wondered why the scene here on the pavilion was not as happy as it would have looked in a painting. Were all those scenes of picnics and outdoor dances, those pictures of people on hotel terraces really lies after all? And the people in them, seemingly so happy, had they really been like Chris and—everybody?

But then, Billy told himself, all that was two or three wars ago, wars and wars ago.

Over his wine, which he suddenly could not drink, Billy eyed his friends, and regretted the fact that none would seriously discuss this question with him. It was an important question. For if we aren't happy, then why—with this sea, and *festa*, and Italy—aren't we? We've chosen to come here, yet there's a kind of unconfessed blame in us against someone, or something we pretend has made us come. Everything I can see now—stars, sea, sand, sky! My name is William Helion, and I'm in Italy.

Stiff as a board, Mrs. Christophe stood spilling her grappa. "He's the right side of my ledger, Chris is!—Oops. Sorry."

"That's all right," said Harness, wiping himself.

"You hear me, Haller, you old shell? Sherry, you know

what I'm about, don't you, doll? Why—I've never even asked Chris the time of day, have I, Chris?" Mr. Christophe said, no; but it was time she did: "Bedtime, Chris." He was embarrassed, and wanted terribly to get her back to the hotel.

Squeezing what triumph she could from his reply, Mrs. Christophe cried, "*See?* And do you know why, Haller? Billy, dear? Everybody? It's because—*to my heart he carries the key*. Remember that, Chris?" He said he did, and Mrs. Christophe began to sing, "Won't you tell him please, to put on some speed—follow my lead—Oh how I need— someone to watch over me. . . ." Mr. Christophe looked up from watching his feet when Chris came to him. After she had given him some of her drink, and together they had put the little green glass on the table, Mrs. Christophe fitted herself beneath his tallness and they walked out through the arch.

Cage had been waiting for them; for they'd not been gone many seconds before the motorcycle roared; roared, roared, then fainted finally away in the distance like a squealing pig someone had let go.

Puccini, thought Billy, listening to the little band playing outside.

"She can be awfully rude at times, Mrs. Christophe," said Harness. "But, then, I suppose it's that grappa."

The Macaroni

Billy pointed toward the music to make it real for his friend.

"Wonderful! Listen, isn't that the motorcycle?"

There was a scream from the street, which made everyone rise from the tables. Whatever had happened . . . !

Three things had, actually. The motorcycle lay, spinning still, on its side; Mr. Christophe and Cage rolled in the road beating each other with their fists; and Mrs. Christophe crouched on her knees before the bright headlights of a huge truck with her face in her hands.

Green, as though he'd run vomiting, Haller was the first one to her. "Handkerchief, please! For Christ's sake, a handkerchief!" He spun halfway around on his buttocks and pulled blindly at the skirt of a woman standing next to him: "Handkerchief!" Then he looked up, and when he did so a ghastly soberness overcame Haller's face, for he saw it was Mrs. Markham's skirt he had hold of. Breaking viciously through what for him might have felt like a trap, Haller then shrieked, "Handkerchief, thief!" Mrs. Markham stared across the pair at Sheridan. "I have none," she managed to say. "I . . .?" Crystal threw down his.

"My nose," Mrs. Christophe whimpered. "Oh Haller, my nose. They've broken my nose."

For a moment Haller took the scene away from Mrs. Christophe. He had fallen beside her, then slid to her on his bottom, not as if he had only one leg, but as though he had none. At the same time there was nothing *good* about Haller; no consolement in his rushing to Mrs. Christophe; no solace.

His drive toward catastrophe had gotten him there first, and now that he held her, he seemed to hate everything. Indeed, Mrs. Christophe struggled to free herself from him before she fainted. "She's passed out," he said, as though it had taken her too long to do so.

Haller was so stretched, so bony at the cheeks, that he reminded Sheridan of a phoenix rising out of ashes that passed for love. Certainly there was no love but love of suffering. There was no meat to the bone, or shell, or echo.

Ironically, they were considered lovers by the crowd.

"I want you both to be quiet," John Harness told Cage and Mr. Christophe, for it was he who separated them, and he was very good about it. "Now go to your wife, Mr. Christophe," he said with wonderful patience. But Christophe was still in a fine rage: "He did it deliberately, I tell you. He deliberately swerved in front of that truck to throw Chris off. I would have gone too, if I hadn't held on to him . . . !"

"*To me!* You held on to those handlebars, you neurotic bastard."

The Macaroni

"Go to your wife, Mr. Christophe."

Cage followed John Harness and Christophe in through a hole in the crowd, through which people ran carrying water. Mrs. Christophe had come to.

"The two of them's just plain mad, John. Just down and out plain goddamned crazy and mad. Why, he tried to kill me just because I said I was leaving!"

Members of the band, taking advantage of intermission, stared down at Mrs. Christophe and Haller. "Now, which is the husband?" "It is the husband holding her." "No, the lover holds her. How shameful! Perhaps it will be the lover, and not the husband, who will pay: unusual." "What a pity it should have happened tonight when there is so much else to see." "Yes, look, the torches are almost gone. Now they are best."

Billy Helion touched one of the older musicians on the arm. "The hill is very beautiful," he said.

"Very beautiful," the old man replied simply. "More beautiful than last year when there was a wind. What a pity this should happen to your friends."

After Mrs. Christophe had been taken to a doctor, the musicians, tapping one another remindfully on the shoulder, went back to their places on the bandstand. The Americans took hold of one another—Crystal of Mrs. Markham, Billy of Haller, John Harness of Leslie, and all went their separate ways. Like Haller, Mrs. Markham said nothing. Walking a little apart from Crystal's chatter, she seemed old and ghastly beige. Sheridan, who had no money to hire a carriage, hoped the eldest sister had not yet gone back to town.

It was impossible for the horse to start while both Sheridan and the Signora were seated together in the carriage. So he descended and walked a little on one side of the horse, while the driver walked on the other. The driver, in fact, walked almost all the way.

"He has had a hard night, the driver," said the eldest sister. For she was conventionally indifferent to the plight of the horse, even though her ancestors had once held him to be as sacred as the wolf. "You will excuse me," she said, when Sheridan had got back in, "if I do not converse with you. I prefer to be silent. A woman's mouth looks as well closed as it does open—better closed, perhaps." And she closed hers firmly.

But as the little carriage lamps wiggled as though to get free, and the horse jogged them almost to sleep through the darkest part of their journey, the Signora sighed unhappily.

"You have found out something; because of the accident?" she asked.

The Macaroni

"Yes," Sheridan whispered, "but it is not worth knowing."

"Perhaps not," she replied. "But to cross over from what was to what is takes courage." Her voice deepened. "I don't think you have it. Forgive me. I have become rough with the café."

She had; but it was hardly the fault of her café. Intuiting another's trouble tends to make us sound more irresponsible than we really are. Certainly to have your secret scooped out of you does leave you rather shaky. They said no more.

Sulking in his corner, Sheridan tried to think of Mrs. Christophe; but she melted from the picture like wax before a fire. He could not feel her pain, as none of us can another's. What remained of the dreadful scene before the headlights of the truck was Haller, and Mrs. Markham: his hand, her skirt, and the word "thief"—thief! This was what he had learned; that very likely she was a thief.

Helpless before this memory, Sheridan was silent, and hoped the eldest sister would understand. She had said he'd found out something. Well, so what? Don't we find out things every day? Not really; hardly at all, in fact. We couldn't stand it if we did. At least I couldn't.

Oh she didn't take the letter! she couldn't! Goddamn Haller!

He continued to stare through the dark at the eldest sister without realizing his deepest feelings, which were, simply, and illogically, that he wished she were stone so that he might safely ask her what to do. Or that she might turn to stone after he had asked, and she had answered. Turning then away from her, he knew he must wait till the light of her café gave back the life in her he liked best.

There in the café, his question, like thousands of other men's questions, would be veiled as statements of likes, dislikes, of complaints and brags; and she, the bartender, would know it for what it was. And maybe, winking in the red wine, glowing blondly in the vermouth, there would be an answer.

Drowsily, Sheridan told the eldest sister that he wished she did think he had a little courage—"because, you see, Signora, one would need it."

"Ah, but you do have a little," she replied indifferently. She yawned, and started up as from a dream: the carriage had stopped. There was a cry for a lamp from the side of the road.

"Your lamp, *idiot!*"

The driver asked who dared call him an idiot, and a short, fierce quarrel broke out between himself and a man he could not see.

"We would use our lamp if we could get it loose.

The Macaroni

Mother of Christ! Wouldn't you know two men would fight like boys at such a time. Wait, here comes another carriage. Keep your lamps, idiot, and may they light your way to the hell you deserve."

Other voices came from the dark. The driver was called a beast, an ass, a wolf, and an idiot so often that he quite dismissed the fact that he'd also been called a fairy. "Who called me idiot?" he asked, walking forward with his lamp. "Who? I am willing to fight!" The lamp was snatched from him, smoking. Then it went out, or seemed to, for the scene turned black as oil.

The eldest sister heaved out of the carriage. "His other lamp. Get it!" Sheridan unhooked the lamp from the side of the carriage. "My carriage! The automobiles! My carriage!" the driver cried. "Who will pay when it is smashed? The Americans do what they want with us and only the opportunists amongst us benefit!" "Quiet, dog. Neapolitan dog. Sicilian!" A scuffle began, which the eldest sister breasted like a swimmer.

The driver and the other man parted; the circle of people around the other lamp opened and showed two women kneeling over another who lay drawn and pregnant on the ground biting into a rag. "Where's the father?" one of the kneelers asked. She stretched her arms out far from her sides and looked up over her shoulder at the faces.

Her voice was thin and silly. "I want to know the father."

"Father to *what?*" the eldest sister gruffly demanded of her. *"You have done nothing!"*

Pulling up her skirt, for she did not forget that it was new and beautiful, and might split, the eldest sister sank with a grunt into the place the other two made for her on the ground. And while Sheridan held the lamp for her to see by, she put her great hands up into the woman and worked them strongly round and round till the sweat dripped from her sharp nose, and the woman, screaming, had blown the rag away.

A subdued carnival of lamps soon lit the side of the road. Men got up out of their carriages and sat under the almond trees like soldiers before an attack. Over and over again their ladies told to the newly arrived the story of what was happening within the circle, which by now had grown immense. "And the American . . . ?" Ah, yes, she was this way also, but had been made so by the lover. He was the young one, naturally.

Though their carriage had been amongst the last to pull up beside the road, both Mrs. Markham and Crystal had established themselves inside the circle—she on one side, and Crystal on the other, close to Sheridan. When the head of the child showed between the woman's legs, Sheridan almost dropped the lamp he was holding. It was

[170]

perhaps the first time in his life he had ever been depended on for anything but pleasure. He writhed till Crystal's hand crouched over his, and till his fingers had given way to Crystal's edging, gentle ones.

The lamplight barely moved as Crystal took complete charge of the lamp, jealous lest the shadows grow bigger, the light less.

The child, red, wrinkled, was born.

There was a hum of delight and appreciation, which crowded like toes at the tip of a pointed shoe.

Taking a deep, exasperated breath, the eldest sister blew into the baby's mouth, then turned it over and smacked its rump till it wailed, till it glimmered, and till it showed it was alive: "How beautiful," was then very simply said.

"*Bravo, Signora. Bravissimo!*"

The words fled the circle. They went gaily doubling themselves like hundreds and hundreds of butterflies of sound up and down, and down and up the road. "*Ancora!*" shouted a joker, and everyone laughed and repeated what he had said, and asked who had said it. "Oh yes, *ancora!*"

Sheridan slipped away, followed by Mrs. Markham. When she joined him out by the carriages, he was reminded of the night they had first crossed the piazza together—as strangers, knowing more about each other than they knew what to do with. "Here's our carriage, Sheridan," said Mrs. Markham, with an air of finality in her voice that Sheridan was rather tempted to attribute to the unsealing effects of wine.

Sinking wearily back into the cushions, Mrs. Markham sighed and closed her eyes. "Oh *ancora, ancora,*" she irritably murmured. "How tiresome they are, how unimaginative," and dozed off to sleep.

PART III: *The Sea Wall*

[*Chapter Ten*]

Lima, Peru
May, 1949

DEAR ALICE:

I have heard through a business associate of the death of Jonathan. I offer, first, my condolences, late though they be; and second, as a possible refuge to you, my home here in Lima.

Sincerely,

JOHN MARKHAM

"Can you picture me retiring to Lima, Sheridan?" Mrs. Markham asked across the luncheon table. It was the day after the *festa,* whose events had been sufficiently exhausting, Mrs. Markham felt, to allow her this beginning of a confidence. Instantly, however, she regretted saying what she had: Lima loomed, and Markham loomed with it. His offer struck her as comical then, and she laughed. "No, don't try," she cried, seeing that Sheridan was experiencing some difficulty in producing a smile. "You're quite right, Sheridan. It's not funny."

And yet it was. What incredible nerve: as if by the window there Markham had passed with just a movement of his lips: "Good day, Alice."

"Do you remember coming in at all last night, Mrs. Markham?" Sheridan asked. "The place was an uproar; people cheered Crystal to his room; wouldn't surprise me if they make him mayor. . . ."

Mrs. Markham, her eyes on the window, replied with a vague, "Remember? Oh goodness yes; but let's not talk of it." Humorously wrinkling a corner of her mouth she gazed at Sheridan with a look of careless play in her face that he had heretofore not seen. "Looking at me and my little history, you'd think, wouldn't you, Sheridan, that I'd led a neat life? But the truth is that I probably could have committed murder without anyone finding me out." She looked at the window again. "Adventurer!" she exclaimed. "Why, there's more of the adventurer even in my shadow than there is in the entire body of some I've known."

"I'm sure there is," said Sheridan. To which "jollying" Mrs. Markham laughed outright. "No you're not sure," she said. "You don't even care. You don't know what you're talking about; and there's no reason that you should know."

Folding Markham's letter away, she rose from the table. Once more her eyes dwelt on the window, as if she were daring the unseen to show itself; as if, for her, there *were* words on the windowpane. "Indeed I do remember last night," she said, as she left Sheridan looking after her. "I recall everything."

Later, in her own room, Mrs. Markham wondered what she had done with Markham's invitation. It was inside her dress, next to her skin, but this she had to wait until she undressed to discover.

For days after hearing from Markham, Mrs. Markham pretended to be still bitter about him. It was a pretense she enjoyed, if only because it offered respite from the dilemma of her friedship with Sheridan. Markham, she tended to remember not as she had last seen him, but as she had seen him first: his eyes blue as this sea. Barely speaking or listening to what Crystal said, Mrs. Markham sat most of the time with that young man on the terraced roof of the *pensione*. These were June days, long and bright; the nights sudden as fireworks.

Crystal talked to her of Africa, rather as Markham had once done of the Caribbean; what Crystal wanted her to do was point toward Africa, thought Mrs. Markham, and off he would go. The day she decided to do so Markham began to appear to her: he came deftly as a breeze in a wittily styled hat. After a week he began to show himself indoors. He exhibited himself and headgear in all doorways but the one to her room. His consideration for her was marked as ever, and Mrs. Markham was not displeased when there evolved between them a game. Rules, which she authored, grew simultaneously with the game itself. One, for example, was that it should be kept secret. There was no need of another person. Actually, however, Mrs. Markham found an extra presence a stimulant, especially since Markham had taken to appearing, with a wink, in a fez!

Slight though all this was, it was the Markhams' final separation. Like humorous spirits they met to draw up a divorce out of the air, to which they agreed with a look, brushing each other as they passed for the last time.

Poor dear! thought Mrs. Markham, when, following on the windy heels of a sirocco, which for a day tinted with

dust the Morabido's silver, Markham showed up looking
the worst for wear, and for the last time, in a coonskin!

Well . . . ! For the moment a sense of loss filled Mrs.
Markham. What she missed was not Markham, then, but
her old bitterness concerning him: had it taken death to
unpin it from her? She thought so. As she lifted her arm in
a good-by gesture to the air her eye was held by a geranium
in cruel-red flower. How base after all to say good-by,
was her forlorn conclusion, when, in the deeper meaning
of things, they had not ever quite said hello. However,
here was Crystal!

He lay asleep in the sun at the foot of Mrs. Markham's
chair. Taking a chance on what consolement he might
offer her, Mrs. Markham reached to rouse the boy, but
then she thought, no: Crystal was better when he slept.
She liked looking at him. His nakedness held perfection
enough to appease the eye, but not, Mrs. Markham
thought, the heart. The heart went hungry.

So instead of hearts, she thought of history, and fancied
Crystal as a sacrifice left over from ancient times; a human
sacrifice from whom all supplicants had centuries ago fled.
Thus he lay in need of an altar, and in need of a god beneath a sky callously emptied of hope, though not of
beauty. All religions must then be dead. How dead, though,
wondered Mrs. Markham, when a boy from—was it De-

troit?—recalls them to me by the lively sleeping look of him? Or was it that she had become a lover of boys? The thought whipped across her mind like a butterfly of ice. Warmed rather than not by this bizarre creature who had led her back again to the heart, Mrs. Markham reached for Crystal, and this time gently roused him.

He sat up with the palms of his hands to his eyes. Like the monkey, his companion remarked to herself, who would see no evil. A rush of cold feeling again informed her that Markham had died, and this time it made her feel unmistakably lonely. "Now what," she hurriedly asked, "about Sheridan?"

"Nothing," Crystal replied. "I just don't like him."

"Ridiculous! Everyone does."

"Well, he doesn't like me, then."

"That too is beside the point. If you like him, he'll like you. He can't avoid affection."

"Cynicism: he doesn't care enough."

True, she supposed, and she said no more. Calm, calm; an endearing calm surrounded her. How content she was.

"Isn't it time for your swim?" she asked.

Crystal rose obediently and pulled his slip of a bathing costume down over his buttocks. A few minutes later he was making his eager mark in the sea. As though, like

Icarus, he'd fallen into it, thought Mrs. Markham, whose deeper feelings were that if Crystal had fallen he had done so to please her. She returned abruptly to the bamboo shelter to get her book, but remembered that Crystal had taken it to her room for her on his way down. He accepted her, she felt, in a way none of the others did.

Like most of us, Mrs. Markham did not know what to do with unsolicited affections; because she could not return them, and thought she should, they oppressed her. Goodness knows, I've enough trouble handling those I want, she irritably thought. However, the beach and sea, when she turned to them again, were empty; the beach as anonymous as a floor in a dream; the sea, silent, speckless; the horizon, voracious. In an instant Mrs. Markham felt herself snap free of her past; strings around herself and Jonathan, angry leashings to Markham, broke and left her with a sense of freedom she despaired of ever using. Never with further honesty could she fear to remember either of them, or hope to restore them in the form of another. They were gone.

"Mrs. Markham! Hi there!" Crystal, sailing a white towel through the air, glistened crossing the shadowless street. But Mrs. Markham, without making a reply, let him pass beneath her into the *pensione*. Untied of old love, she took the final, decisive turn to the new, and for the first time saw Sheridan as a person totally apart from Jonathan. From this flowered her plan. If it succeeded she would want nothing else; but should it fail, then she would want nothing.

It was from the island's farthermost point, the sea wall, that Mrs. Markham envisaged their departure, hers, Sheridan's, up through the Mediterranean to some inland city, where they would live out the rest of her days in enduring friendship. Evenings she strolled with Sheridan to the powerhouse and back, while the vessel lay lighted, wavering beside them in the bay. Her plan was an extenuation of these strolls, as real, as inevitable. How big the little steamboat—their vessel—was to her; yet she had scarcely noticed it till now. Now the sight and sound of it would be a pleasure. So are things made grand and luminous by the hopes we place in them.

"Mrs. Markham . . . !"

"Sheridan! How close you sounded."

He stood with just half of him showing out of the dark stairwell.

"Give me your hand, Mrs. Markham."

"Yes," she said, doing so, "but not so fast. Remember, Sheridan, that I've been in the sun."

Descending with Sheridan to the dining room, Mrs.

The Sea Wall

Markham inquired directly about the steamboat she had been seeing every afternoon, and whose departing whistle she'd heard every morning at five. *La Méditerranée,* this was its name. Wasn't that whistle a bore? No, Mrs. Markham liked it; she adored the fact that, due to there being no pier here as there was in Corvo, one had to row out to the vessel to board it. *La Méditerranée.* "But Mrs. Markham, it's been there all the time."

"Yes, every day. Imagine. We never know, do we?"

Lima again, thought Sheridan. For despite Mrs. Markham's having made bitter fun of her invitation from that Peruvian city, Sheridan was now convinced that she had not meant it. Obviously there had been some reshuffling of her past which caused her to dwell on it; and, as Sheridan had somewhat jealously begun to believe, given her a coming-and-going desire to go back to it. Why this should have affected Mrs. Markham in her feelings for him, he could not guess; it was fairly painful, the feeling he had of boring her. Amazing, he could ever have considered her to have once come so close to him as to steal. Cold comfort though it was, Sheridan now realized Mrs. Markham had been the one person in his life most seriously concerned for him; his interest in finding out why she had lost it, and where exactly he had failed her, tortured him.

If ever he had to say just what it was he did these days,

Sheridan would perhaps have recalled those times his mind had been busy with plans, and not the other, more numerous hours spent dreaming with his eyes open. His greedy anticipation of mealtime he would remember with the oppressive heat, but not how he sat perspiring on the edge of his bed after swatting flies. This, his one pleasure besides eating, Mrs. Markham innocently heightened for him by mentioning the noise he made doing it. If it bothered her he would not kill them any more? Mrs. Markham said it did not bother her in the least. Nothing did, he thought; and so the capricious hunt continued. An old *Life* magazine was his weapon. It lay constantly beside him with his towel, which he would whip around him when Antonia knocked.

Sheridan would easily recall how he'd worn nothing, but not how his body refused to come alive to him sexually. For during these long days, these swollen hot nights, sex was a memory to him. He felt impotent. His test flights, as he thought of them, were taken solo before a mirror: landing, he would wonder if he'd been up at all.

His last letter from Rome was so disinterested that even Cooper, sensing this, had wound up with an apology. Sheridan concluded from its tone that his friend was absorbed in his work. Reduced to Antonia, he flirted with her: Letters? Any letters for me? till the sight of his own boredom reflected in the servant's eyes stilled him. Like many who do not pay their way, Sheridan had a strongly developed sense of those who did; and though Antonia herself had no economic power, she was connected to the Morabidos, on whom he depended for the food he had come so to love, to say nothing of their vast brass bed in which he spent so much of his time. Otherwise he might not have taken Antonia seriously.

Sheridan was respectful about money. He himself did not want it, but he owed it to himself to be near it. For it was then his responsibilities began. Helion and Cooper had money. Haller's paintings sold. John Harness was rich; while the Christophes, living relentlessly above their means, nevertheless had financial foundations. Perhaps it was because Crystal was poor that Sheridan had not become friendly with him. Benefiting from an accident of war, Crystal lived off a government pension, which was next to nothing. Next to nothing was less than nothing to Sheridan; a dead end. Whereas money offered continuity, poverty was incapable of offering anything but itself. Quite probably Sheridan would not have come to feel Mrs. Markham's proximity had she not been a woman of fairly certain means.

In the dining room Mrs. Markham nibbled complacently the readheaded fish which she had once so actively loathed:

"No, this will do perfectly, thank you." Eating little, saying scarcely a word, she discriminated as to quantity alone. She was absorbed, absolved; a saint, so Sheridan decided, without a belief. Extending her hand to Antonia, Mrs. Markham plunged her fingers into the servant's bird-nest swirl of hair. "Miss Fish," she airily murmured. "Sheridan, have you met our little Miss Fish?" Antonia went dry at this. No matter her affection for Mrs. Markham, one could see by her abrupt departure to the kitchen that she had not relished being referred to as "Signorina Pesce." Italians are strict about differences. They are notably aware of the differences between themselves and the animals they serve, or those that serve them.

"Didn't you," Sheridan asked, "use to call her something beside Antonia?"

"Yes," Mrs. Markham replied, "I did call her something else. But she annoyed me."

"She adores you."

"Perhaps that's it."

Which eliminated Antonia; and himself as well, Sheriridan felt.

Together with Crystal they went that evening to Billy Helion's for cocktails. The cocktails turned out to be rather spiteful: there was no gin in them. Mrs. Markham, oppressed by the sweet and heavy air of the house, stepped immediately on Haller's cat. And because it was the kind of doomed gathering it was—markedly unsuccessful from the first—there was as much to-do about the little accident as was possible.

After the last boring cat story had been told, and Mrs. Markham had lowered from her nose her handkerchief, which smelled vilely of yellow soap, Billy brought out a postcard from Venice, from Mrs. Christophe. "'Harry's bar every night.'" Billy read. "'Pigeons and gold every day. Love you dolls!'" He looked up from the postcard, ashamed, rather, that he had bothered to read it: it brought the motorcycle accident depressingly up to the minute. "I've always felt miserable in Venice myself," Billy lied, by way of apology. "Do you like it, Mrs. Markham?"

"What *do* I smell?" she asked, for it had got worse.

"Eucalyptus leaves," Billy told her. "I start my fires with them."

"Didn't they in Peru?" Mrs. Markham wondered. She half rose from the sofa with her hands out to Sheridan, who assisted her. The others, who had been sitting so close as to smother her, she felt, got up too; though she was not sure, for she had shut her eyes. Billy went out with them to the terrace. "Perhaps," Mrs. Markham said breathlessly, "there weren't any after all . . . ?"

"Eucalyptus trees?" Billy asked. "I don't know. I've never been. Is it Inca, or Aztec, Peru?"

"I don't see what's Peru to do with it!" Sheridan exclaimed irritably.

"Sheridan's right," said Mrs. Markham. "Nothing to do with it at all; especially since I know it wasn't Peru anyway. Goodness! it almost smothered me, that smell. Yet you like it, don't you, Mr. Helion?"

"I love it." Billy was more adamant than he needed to be.

Mrs. Markham stared at a huge eucalyptus throwing its sheep dog of a shadow clear across Billy's garden. Through it there were blue and powdered pieces of the view. "That's nice," she said, meaning just such an opening in the lovely tree. "But you don't see the sea, do you?—You know, I never thought I'd want to leave here, but now I do."

She had withdrawn obsessively from everything but her plan for departure; but Sheridan, because he did not know this, was hurt by what Mrs. Markham had said about wanting to leave the island. Mrs. Markham felt strangely tonight that the morning when they would row out together to *La Méditerranée* was soon due to arrive. Till it did, everything else was an intrusion; every minute a needled barricade.

Placing a detaining hand on Sheridan, she smiled at

Billy Helion. "I hope," she said, "that I'm not minding the heat. Heat's one thing I've never minded. Smells, yes. Have you ever been to Barbados, Mr. Helion?"

Crystal said next morning the drinks had given him heartburn. Mrs. Markham wondered how so. Hadn't they remained untouched as jars in a pharmacist's window, their contents, though decorative, mysterious to all but their maker? She preferred not to talk about it; hoped, indeed, not to have to see either young man again. Way up the mountain one made out a donkey; and out on the sea was a single fishing boat. It was a beautiful day, a day without edge or end, suspended in space like a golden apple. Someone, Crystal felt, had put the fishing boat on the sea's smooth surface to prove that beneath it was water. He sank to his knees silently as a rope. "Mrs. Markham, why don't you come with me to Africa?" It was only an idea. "Why not?" Crystal insisted with laughing wonder in his voice. For however lightly he had asked, he was surprised, even puzzled, that Mrs. Markham could have answered so quickly without saying a word. "We must be very serious," Mrs. Markham said at last. Then she told him about Sheridan.

Sheridan whipped his towel around him and let Antonia in. She followed him to the bed. His hands, when he drew her to him, trembled with excitement, but it was not till after he had questioned her about the letter that he realized he did not want to know; he particularly did not want her to inform on Mrs. Markham. The letter—the ridiculous Maughamish letter. Christ, how he loathed it! Antonia, however, had had enough of being on two sides at once; Sheridan might just as well have tried to stop a wave from breaking over him as stop her now. Yet, for a few minutes, that is just what he did do. Taking Antonia by the hand, he led her out to the beach.

It was white noon. And they were out in it when no one else was, like lovers. Open to each other, they were closed to everyone else, so it did not matter where they walked, or who saw them, or even why they walked where they did: bigger than either was the secret they shared. It was this that led them.

Sheridan, who had dressed while she watched him, wore only his chamois shorts. No shoes, nor did Antonia, for hers had been worn out at the *festa*. Though romantic, she did not weep, but wisely reserved her tears for less eventful days. She had been bombed out: airplanes were birds to Antonia till then, and children were people like oneself. Afterwards, of course, children were nothing. When one stands lost where the third floor of one's house had once been, what good are children? Ugly. So Antonia walked in step with Sheridan, not hand in hand, but closely all the same, as a comrade should, over the hot blond sand, and down at last along the edge of the cool water.

There was not even a bird. A fishing boat was there, but they would not have seen it had they not climbed the granite steps to the sea wall. Yes, Signora Markham did have the letter. It was in her bedside table drawer un-opened as the day she'd demanded Antonia give it to her: "It was my pleasure to bring you your letters, Signor Sherry. Forgive me?" She raised her hands together a little ways out from her chest. "Forgive me?" she asked, but of course he had not the time to say whether he did or not.

He had only to turn and say so as he descended the steps to the beach, but he did not. Left alone, Antonia coldly reviewed the past half-hour. The fact that she had now witnessed Sheridan's nakedness, and that Mrs. Mark-ham had perhaps not, gave the child a cruel sense of achievement. She remained motionless, her hands before her still, her gray eyes a shade disdainful.

Then, just as Signor Sherry turned the corner to the *pensione,* Antonia unclasped her little hands and brought them together again. Otherwise she did not move.

[*Chapter Eleven*]

M̲r̲s̲. M̲a̲r̲k̲h̲a̲m̲ had only just slipped into her dressing gown when Sheridan knocked. The draft from the hallway, when she opened her door, caused her shutters to blow wide apart; the room, which she had wanted dark, was now made hideously bright with sunlight: "I must keep one or the other locked all the time," she impatiently explained, "else they all blow open in the slightest breeze. Come in. How perspiring you are."

Sheridan passed her swiftly into the room, then stood with his back to her, facing the dazzling balcony.

"Shut those shutters, Sheridan; I can barely make you out."

"I have something to say, Mrs. Markham," he said without turning to her. "I'm afraid I'll have to be horribly serious."

"But it's too hot, or haven't you noticed? Where in the world have you been? You're dripping!"

"I wish," he said, with an even more fatal absence of humor, "that you weren't here."

"Oh I do too," Mrs. Markham replied; "but I'm afraid there's no place I can go—not for the moment anyway. You see, I'm being pursued!" Catching her throat lightly in her hand, she threw back her head and laughed. "Do you know, Sheridan, that that Crystal just asked me to go to Africa with him? He made me feel," she explained, wide-eyed, and askance, as though into a dreadful morning mirror, "oh, so assailable. I suppose that was why I told him what I did. He rather frightened me."

"Forgive me, Mrs. Markham, but I haven't come to gossip."

"But you never have, Sheridan! And for that I can't forgive you. I feel you do gossip, though, but never with me. It's a lonely feeling, that."

The Sea Wall

"Lonely?" Sheridan turned to her at last, but because he'd been staring unnaturally hard into the sunlight, Mrs. Markham was for the moment a pink haze to him.

"Lonely, yes," she smilingly replied. "Is it so strange to you that I should feel that?"

Lifting her arms she leisurely removed her earrings—pearls she had gotten for Jonathan to give her on one of her birthdays. "I'd forgotten them."

"Have you also forgotten the letter which once you took from Antonia—by accident?"

"There!" she suddenly cried, "we've missed lunch." She remained quite still, however, and with her back to him; her hands rested on the closet shelf on which she had placed the jewels.

"By accident, no," she replied, facing him. "I took it knowing quite well what it was about, though I pretended at the time that I did not.—Now, we must be sensible about this, Sheridan. Between ourselves, it was nothing to have done, but between society and ourselves . . . ? Well, about that I wouldn't know; nor, as a matter of fact, would you. We are both of us outsiders, and there is no good pretending that we are not. It would have been ridiculous of me, for instance, to have allowed myself to be shocked by that boy's suggestion that I mother him to Africa: I've laid myself open to such things; but not"—she smiled—"so very open that I could be 'touched' by his need. Frankly I loathed him, as I do myself about this mess, and as I do you, rather, in that you are so wildly geared to making the most out of it you can. I warned you I was tired, and irritable, and hot, but you would not listen. However"— she moved forward through the glare—"I suppose it was time you reminded me of it."

Sheridan, smiling at the nerve with which she intended to carry the thing off, stepped aside to let Mrs. Markham get at her bedside table. She had no sooner touched it, however, than her real nervousness manifested itself, and she knocked over the lamp. Sheridan picked it up.

"Now go sit down, Mrs. Markham," he quietly told her.

"I mean to, certainly . . . !" she replied, glancing suspiciously at him. "But first——"

Sheridan pressed her firmly away from the table.

"What *are* you doing, Sheridan? Didn't you promise to be rational about this?"

"I didn't promise a thing."

"Well, perhaps not; but I see little point in your rooting in my things."

"I have no interest in your things, Mrs. Markham."

"You're right," she said, with an abrupt shake of her head. "I admit it was a stupid and pointless thing to have done. What more can I say now than that?"

"You might say you're sorry."

Mrs. Markham turned abruptly away. "Take it," she said.

Yet when Sheridan did open her drawer and take the letter, Mrs. Markham experienced a sense of loss far in excess of that on which she had counted. Piercing what hope there remained to her, it pointed not simply to her loss of the letter, which, after all, was of no real consequence, but to the hideous loss of Sheridan himself: *He would go away without her.*

What she felt then was the simultaneous rising in her of both laughter and tears. Her breath shot from her as if she'd been struck on the back. Horrified, Mrs. Markham considered she had snorted, which indeed she had. She felt composed of fat and nothing else. However, she was pleased that she had not wept. This, at least, told her she had no new thing to learn from defeat. She felt better then; more herself. She felt dry, hard; thin as she had ever felt, as, raising her shoulders like a cloak of bones against Sheridan, she sank into bed. There, she was once more overcome by a feeling of heaviness: her eyes rested sullenly on the letter which hung down from his fingers between his legs.

"Would you," she asked, nodding in the direction of her closet, "like something to drink?"

"And now," she said, after they had tasted their drinks, and Sheridan had pocketed his letter, "you'll go away, won't you?" She thought of the picture of St. Vitus on the wall behind her, and of waking up to it day after day. The lonely pain of this was more real to her than anything. "Really, Sheridan," she softly inquired, "I still don't see why you made such a fuss?"

"Would it mean anything to you, Mrs. Markham, if I explained that the letter contains money? The money I needed before I could pay my bills and leave."

"Then," she said, nodding her head drowsily again, "then I was right."

"About my going away?"

"Yes. Now smoke a cigarette. I—I miss the smell. Has the stupid cat got your tongue? What are you thinking of?"

Stirring, Sheridan looked sharply at her, then he looked away. "Do you really want to know?" he asked.

Mrs. Markham raised her hands; frowned. "Not really," she said; "not at all, actually."

"I'm thinking of what a friend of mine used to tell me when I was a kid. He was a church organist; asthmatic; wore an incredible wig. 'If anything ever happens to me, Sherry' he used to say, 'I want you to beat it. I don't want you hanging around the Village thinking I've let you down.

Just remember,' he'd say, 'that dying will be a hell of a letdown for me, who's never been any nearer Mother Earth than Central Park; and then it was so dark in those days, my dear, that I didn't know black from white.' That was a little joke of his—that about the park. Then he'd tell me to go get the avocados. 'I think they're about ripe,' he'd say. I used to hope he would have finished that business about dying; but always, somewhere in the middle of the avocado, he'd say, 'Now remember what I've told you, Sherry lad. Why, they'd run a looker like you ragged in a Reform.' I can still hear his breath wheezing around the corners of his teeth. I pitied myself for living with him. Then one winter morning I found him dead by the window; the part of his face that wasn't covered by the wig was the same color as the pavement outside. I didn't touch him. All I heard, and all I thought about, was what he'd so often told me. It was as though four radios in each corner of the room were tuned in to him, and he was saying over and over, 'If anything ever happens to me, kid, I want you to beat it.' "

Though Mrs. Markham said nothing to all this, her silence seemed to say a great deal: Wait, he'll come around. He's not so different from Jonathan.

"Don't you see you loved me?" Sheridan broke out. "And it wasn't the kind you might think it was, either.

I mean you loved me the way young people love one another. I don't know what you feel now. Superior, I suppose, and wondering: Just what is this fool doing in my room. You adored me. You've had me, and I never knew till now that you had. *Look:*" The sound of the buttons from his shorts pebbling across the tiles so exhilarated Sheridan that he struck with his glass at the picture of St. Vitus and broke it. *"Look at me!"*

Mrs. Markham did.

"That," she dryly commented, "would be all you know."

"Not all, Mrs. Markham. You underestimate me."

He undressed her easily. Nothing seemed real, however, neither her raised garment, nor her flesh. Though the comfort was cold—against her Sheridan felt this—it was nevertheless comfort, and he wanted as much of it as was there. All but Mrs. Markham's intelligent eyes was passive, and they did something unusual, they begged. Yet for all her humility, she proved not Sheridan's vigor, but his lack of it, and he began to fumble.

He dreamed for hot crowded seconds of haven with Mrs. Markham as her lover, till her eyes roused him silently to the fulfillment of what he had begun to do. Then he fumbled; then, instead of feeling Mrs. Markham's body, Sheridan saw it. There seemed to be not only eyes in his head, but eyes on his nipples as well, and eyes on his

knees, and no pressing could close them, no airless dark
would make them blind. Instructing him to further examination, they refused to close and let him do the deeper
thing.

It was, in its way, a perfect body, Mrs. Markham's, for
it had not really been used, only preserved. It was slug-
white. Her breasts, which had never been full, were sur-
prisingly like those of a young person. The stomach was
flat. It was a body that had never been let have its way.
Skirting all real contact, it had missed too much to be
able to experience surprise now. Nothing had happened
to it, nothing would, nothing could. Yet according to the
fashions of the day it was a stylish body. Dressed, it
moved; and dressed it pretended to be more alive than it
was. It lent itself to killed things; to plucked cotton and
dyed wool, to the silk from the worm, and to the tender
pelt of the seal; but living flesh it was unable to wear.

It refused to be outraged.

Passion—though of that there was not an ounce in
either Mrs. Markham or Sheridan—it might have bent
back with a witticism, but there was not even that. Too
close for wit, incapable of passion, they parted. How cool
and quiet the room seemed then: even the bed failed to
give them away, for it showed Sheridan scarcely a wrinkle.
Only the glass he had smashed told him he was not al-

together impotent. It showed Sheridan what he might have done had he been all arm and fist and nothing else. Teased again into expectancy, he dreamed once more of fulfillment, but this time he knew it was a dream: to have become Mrs. Markham's lover, if only it had not involved this nakedness, would have solved everything. Instead, they were back with a difference where they had begun.

"It's an awful trick to have been played on us," both might have said; but it was their bodies, not their tongues, that were at present the talkers, and their bodies asked to be covered. This, Mrs. Markham failed to heed. The garment remained up where Sheridan had put it, as though it were now concluded that she had little left either to show or to hide. Physically naïve as she certainly was, forgetful as she had always been of her body, she did well to show no shame. Anyway her mind was on other things.

"And you, Sheridan?" she asked with surprising tenderness. "Haven't you rather done the opposite? Haven't you overestimated yourself?"

Startled by the casual sound of her voice, Sheridan eyed Mrs. Markham with breathless acquiescence. "For the moment I suppose I did, yes."

"Exactly. Now, if my limited experiences tell me that the moment, and all its perhaps marvelous possibilities, have passed, what, I wonder"—she smiled—"must yours be telling you?"

The Sea Wall

His, Sheridan felt, told him nothing. For though she did not yet recognize what she had done, Mrs. Markham had drained him dry of experience. He felt a boy again, hating her as he had never been privileged to hate anyone in his life before. Indeed, it was as though he had had no life before. So he said nothing, and Mrs. Markham was pleased.

"Don't be maudlin, Sheridan," she cynically murmured. "Men so often are about these things. All this, you must see, is quite unbelievable. Its only believability rests in the fact that it failed to come off. When all's said, though," she laughingly ended, "you're not half so defeated as I am denied. So come let's say good-by for now."

"One thing, Mrs. Markham . . ."

Turning, Mrs. Markham perched herself up at the foot of the bed to watch the vessel round the sea wall, let down its white anchor in the blue bay.

"Do you," Sheridan asked, gathering up his shorts, "know this, that I hope never to see you again?"

Mrs. Markham folded down into the bed like a piece of cloth. In doing so she struck her head against the bedpost. "It's nothing," she said, and waved him away. "Please, just lock me in, then slip the key back under the door. Thank you."

He did not reply to Antonia when she called him for

dinner. "Signor Sherry"—she tapped—"are you there?" Her voice rose when she called Mrs. Markham. There was no reply. Later, Sheridan locked his door and fled through the sudden dark to the roof.

The power plant had failed; all over town the lights had gone out. Cries of humor and alarm rose up from the surrounding houses. To hear the Signora Morabido shouting below you'd think the electrical accident had affected only the *pensione*: "Was it not enough you strolled off at noon to the beach like a crazy duchess, but now you insist on keeping me in the dark? Turn on the gaslight, orphan!"

The town, finding its way back to reality by candle, wavered as though it were its own reflection. There was a hiding moon. Somewhere someone played a flute.

"Forgive me," Sheridan abruptly murmured. "You must forgive me."

"Forgive me Father for I have sinned! For what, Sherry? How deliciously contrite you sounded." It was Billy Helion; he and Haller emerged from the stairwell pointed as cypresses.

"Billy's birthday," Haller explained, removing his party hat. "We've brought you a piece of the cake."

He put his hat on Sheridan.

"Why, look, Billy, he's dressed in a suit!"

The Sea Wall

"We sent somebody to ask you to dinner, Sherry, but they made a mistake and asked Crystal instead. Did you know he's leaving?"

"Really?" Sheridan tilted the hat at a casual angle.

"Yes, tomorrow. We wondered if it had anything to do with you?"

"Mrs. Markham . . . ? Mrs. Markham . . . ?" Crystal was calling. Barefooted, shirtless, he climbed out of the stairwell. "I thought I heard voices," he said.

"I should hope so!" Haller laughed. "The place is like Halloween tonight!"

"It's the lights. I was packing when they went off. Oh, by the way, Sherry, I'm leaving tomorrow. Here's so long if I don't see you again." He shook hands all around, then backed away into the dark.

"What *is* he doing, the little spook?" Billy whispered. It was annoying the way Crystal stood off somewhere by himself.

"Hearing voices again, I guess," said Haller. "I wonder what's kept him here so long anyway?"

"Mrs. Markham . . . ?"

"Jesus! but he's frightening. Does he think she's a cat? God knows I do!"

"He's calling down to her balcony," Sheridan piously explained.

"Can't he go down?" Haller asked. "Why don't you try her door, Crystal?"

There was a slight pause during which the flute music whirled hilariously up through the air.

"I did," said Crystal. "It's locked."

Lowering his voice, Haller laughingly pointed a finger at Sheridan. "Oh Sherry, Sherry, you are the reason for his leaving us, aren't you? Did he try to take her from you?"

"Are you going to sue me for alienation of affections?" asked Billy. "At any rate, take the cake, and consider yourself forgiven."

"And this . . . ?"

"That no," said Haller, taking the hat from him. "This is to be a keepsake. You see, Sherry, we decided to buy the house today."

"Come back with us and look at it," said Billy. "It seems to have altogether changed now that it's ours."

"Say something, Sherry. Wish us luck with it, anyway."

"Oh, but I do wish you luck. I'm sorry, but for the minute the idea of it made me feel so separate."

"From us? But you can always come stay. Come now, if you like."

Touched, Sheridan replied that he'd take them up on that someday. "But for now, shall we go?"

Leading the way downstairs, he closed the door of the

pensione softly behind him and walked a few yards up the hill beside the bay, the lighted boat. Then he stopped and whirled around with the piece of cake held over his head.

"Hey Billy! Happy birthday, you old bastard!"

[*Chapter Twelve*]

ON THE WHARF at Corvo there is a chocolate-colored Christ with an electric light bulb in his hand. Near it a few people waited for the boat. They stood apart from one another till the sun rose and warmed them, then they turned their backs to the water and watched the bus coming down out of the hills carrying on its top a great mess of bandaged suitcases and bundles. Through its windows the travelers stared, anxious lest the boat had come and gone without them.

First out of the bus was a lovely lean girl of about fifteen who, rushing through the crowd to the edge of the wharf, stood, her hands clasped behind her, watching the approaching vessel flirtatiously part the waves. *"La Méditerranée,"* she cried, turning to a woman who had followed slowly behind her. The girl's hair caught beneath her chin for an instant like a helmet of meshed gold. All eyes were on her. *"Ah Mamma mia."* She threw her arms about the woman, who in her turn was accompanied by six nuns, all of whom stood like stubby black candles; several of them were weeping.

"An angel!" said a loud, tough-looking woman in a candycane-striped blouse. "Beautiful, and also an angel!"

An Englishwoman in wool considered it a crime.

"You mean to say you don't think it a crime, David, that girl going off to bury herself in a convent?"

David had not been thinking of the girl. "Notice," said he, "how Italians let things go. Now take that Christ, the electric bulb, I mean. And what a damned awful color!"

"I do *so* love it!" she confessed, furious.

"Give me a little blessing, dear one." An old knot of a woman rubbed herself against the blond girl. "Come on, sweetheart, the tiniest blessing will do me."

"Behave yourself," one of the nuns admonished the old woman. "Why, you see she's only a girl. What's got into you?"

"Only a girl, is she!" The old one laughed, wagging her morsel of a bottom. "What was any saint but only a girl, a boy, before you people got hold of them?" Flopping fancifully down on the wharf, she wailed, "Robbers! Don't take her from us. Robbers!"

The nun gave her an affectionate pat on the head and pulled her to her feet. "Now come and say good-by properly. Here's the boat with not a seat left for her, you can be sure; though little she'll mind, being what she is."

The gangplank soon sagged with travelers; beside it, his duffel bags at his feet, stood Crystal. Sheridan shot by him to the coffee lounge, which contained a bishop receiving with climbing eyes the public confessions of two women masked in sun glasses.

Crystal set out to join Sheridan, for he had seen him come aboard. Adjusting with nervous expectation his sole acquisition from the island—a blue velvet beret—he waited, however, till *La Méditerranée* had made its last stop and he had paid homage to the island. Watching the last pink disappearing wharf of the last town, then, across the lavender water, the island itself, the young traveler was for the moment sincerely convinced that he would give anything to go back.

"*San Antonio, per favore, San Antonio.*" A little sunrouged monk shook his begging box at all but the "regulars," then stood in the slippery breeze pleasuring his eyes with the closely passing islands. Other islands, thought Crystal, contributing for luck, some with old pillboxes set like cheeses on their farthest, most delicate points. At the door to the lounge he turned and looked back, but where the island should have been there were only clouds now rolling north.

"What'd you do, Sherry, take the bus? I didn't know there was one so early."

Picking up speed, the vessel shivered; a woman, too stout to have attempted so far a dive, fell into the bishop's ring. "Ayee, what heat!" moaned another, who, rising head and shoulders over everybody on her rhinestone-and-emerald-studded platforms, left to Crystal her seat beside Sheridan.

Sheridan ordered coffee.

"I walked. Ten miles it must be. I ache."

"Did the lights never come on?" Crystal asked him. "I stayed up on the roof after you all left. And then—well, it was time. Oh, and by the way, Sherry, will you, when you get back, tell Mrs. Markham good-by for me?"

"Sugar?"

"Please. I couldn't very well have barged in on her at five in the morning, could I?"

"Do you know Naples?" Sheridan asked. "How long are you staying?"

The Sea Wall

"Three days. My boat sails on the twenty-seventh. But you aren't staying, are you, Sherry?"

"Maybe. Would you like a brandy? Two brandies," Sheridan said, giving his coffee cup to the waiter. "Hold my seat; I'll be right back."

The bishop had fallen asleep.

"If I have said it once—" said one of the women with sun glasses.

"Once!" cried her friend.

"—I have," continued the other, flicking a fly off the bishop, "said it a thousand times."

"Thousands and thousands of times, dear, as I have said to *mine*."

"Yes, from the day I married him, that my religion was mine. 'Let it support you then,' he said only last night."

"Are we arrived?" the bishop blandly inquired of one, then the other of his masked companions. "Is it Naples, children?"

"What are you going to do in Naples?" Crystal asked, giving Sheridan the brandy he had been patiently holding for him.

"Oh, eat, shop, go to a good hotel. Why don't you come along? I've got the money, so you won't have to worry. If you are worried, that is."

"No, I'm not worried, but I do miss it all, don't you?

Only you're going back. I'm envious of you, in a way."

"Let's go outside. Shall I help you with one of those bags?"

Sun-logged mothers, like big-bosomed birds of printed silk, guarded their daughters more urgently, for they were almost there. "We're almost there, David, and that wretched girl has done nothing but look *back*!"

"*San Antonio per favore* . . ." Absent-mindedly the little monk went doing his rounds again. His eyes were as bleached as a sailor's; yet how different he looked from the hundreds who this minute were staring his way from all over an American battleship bewitched this side of Vesuvius, hundreds and hundreds of creamy-capped sailors.

"And to think," said Crystal, "that I may never go back."

Between boats blaringly bound for Capri, *La Méditerranée* docked.

"But really, I'm having a wonderful time."

Sheridan steered him toward a taxi. Once inside, Crystal began twisting for the name of the hotel Haller had given him on a slip of paper. "I had it right here."

"You said you wouldn't worry, remember?" Sheridan reminded him, laughing.

"Oh no, I won't worry. I said I'm having a wonderful time, and I am. I'm tickled we met."

Sheridan gave the name of the hotel to the taxi man,

then threw his legs thoughtfully across the duffel bags. Might he tell Crystal about Mrs. Markham? he wondered. Would Crystal be still enough? Wouldn't it be rather like getting a collar on a puppy dog?

"I adore traveling," he suddenly exclaimed, "don't you?"

The Signora Morabido had brought to Mrs. Markham a doctor and two appalling policemen. Mrs. Markham, who had also traveled, was thankful she had done so only in a dream. She had lain through what seemed to her hours of dawn watching a window crossed by the splintered shadow of a winter tree; a dog had barked; the studio door slammed continuously.

It was a dream, of course, but the idea of such misplacement was hideous. It was still dark then. Grateful to be where she was, Mrs. Markham had fallen back to sleep, her hand curled about the whisky glass, which was the second thing Signora Morabido noted after letting herself in. The first had been the key Sheridan had slipped back under Mrs. Markham's door.

"I dreamed I was in New England, my home," Mrs. Markham told her.

"No, Signora, you are safe with us. The brute has fled."

"I must say"—Mrs. Markham smiled at the doctor—"that I'm relieved I am with you."

The doctor ordered her a sedative, then inquired whether or not the welt on her forehead gave her pain.

"None at all," Mrs. Markham replied. "I am perfectly well, and would just like my tea."

The police, one fat, the other pencil-thin, stood beneath St. Vitus.

"St. Rocco," said one.

"No," said the other, "it is St. Vitus."

"What's he doing with the dog, then? It was St. Rocco always with the dog, was it not, Signora?"

"God knows!" the Signora Morabido replied. "But how he does *bulge* since the accident."

Mrs. Markham asked, had they to make a racket?

"How nervous she is!" cried Signora Morabido joyfully.

"He might have murdered her," said the round policeman, beginning furiously to write things down. "Writing is very difficult," he explained to the Signora Morabido. "The heat makes most things difficult," she told him, wondering, however, if he wasn't handsome.

"What a fine room," said the thin policeman, who openly considered himself the Interesting One. "Very spacious."

"Thank you," replied Signora Morabido, glancing at him. "Is the table all right to write on?" she said to the other, for it turned out he was handsome after all. What legs! "Such a little table," she cried. "Look! It hardly holds you!"

The Sea Wall

"Tea," said the doctor, "is just the thing."

Signora Morabido hurried *him* out, then ordered coffee for the police. The Interesting One asked if his might be flavored with milk. The other took a busy sip, then handed Signora Morabido his cup on his way to Mrs. Markham.

"How long have you been here at the *pensione*, Signora?"

"Four months."

"And how long has the man been here?"

"Signor Sherry he means, Signora."

"Three months," Mrs. Markham replied.

"And how long have you known one another?"

Mrs. Markham lifted herself on her elbow and nodded at her door. "Please go, Signora, and take these men with you. If you disturb me once more with this nonsense, I shall report you to your husband."

After they left, Mrs. Markham wept, for though they had closed her shutters and carried away the broken glass, they still had not brought her tea.

Shielding his face from the blowing pongee draperies, Crystal fell back into one of the beds: "I've never been in a place like this." With his black sweater, and sneakers, his rubber-smooth tanned skin, and blue velvet beret, he had caused a murmuring sensation in the lounge downstairs. A tiny playground of a wharf belonging to a yacht club floated in the water across from the hotel. Sheridan watched from above its blue-and-gold pennants strung for the moment between two attendants; beyond them a sail went up white with surprise.

"Shall we have another drink?" he asked Crystal.

Quietly Crystal remarked that he was still dazed: "I think you're crazy, Sherry, coming here!"

They held up, later, their disconcertingly red-stemmed martini glasses. Sheridan, smiling thoughtfully over his, said, "Happy days, kid."

"The man," Crystal echoed abruptly, "says happys days." He rolled over on his face, his glass tilting from his hand like a scooped-out rose.

"You must be excited about leaving?" Sheridan asked sympathetically.

"Terribly! I feel nothing can break me now. Did you ever feel that way, Sherry?"

"I suppose I have; it's a wonderful feeling."

Crystal came over to the window and put his arm in a careless gesture of friendship about Sheridan's shoulder.

"In a funny way," he said, "I was stuck on that island, but I liked it enormously. I must remember to send Mrs. Markham a card."

"Are you going to stay in Tangier?" Sheridan asked.

"I'm not sure; there are so many possibilities for me, aren't there?"

The Sea Wall

"If I were you I'd go down through Spain: Madrid, Granada, Algeciras. You'd love it."

"I'm sure. But I've already got my ticket. Look, another sail!"

"Seville too!" Sheridan went on.

"Sherry," Crystal said, giving him a cigarette, "I think you're more excited about the trip than I am. Maybe the three of us can meet somewhere."

"I am excited," Sheridan admitted. He was; he saw no reason not to go along on the trip with Crystal. Standing here at the window looking out over the bay, he had begun to feel he could do anything, go almost anywhere; all he needed, actually, was another handout from Cooper. "I like going over people's trips with them, don't you?" His hunch was that he was going. "Let's have lunch sent up. You order while I take a shower."

"What do you want to eat, Sherry?" Crystal called out when the waiter arrived with the menu.

"Anything but avocados!"

"They don't have any avocados."

"Good! I said anything *but*! What towels!" Wrapping himself in a huge bath towel, which he decided to take along with him to Africa, Sheridan sat down to lunch.

"I can't think of a better point of departure for me than this place, Sherry. Real chicken salad, almost real mayonnaise. You can't believe how grateful I am that I met you."

"I'm much more glad I met you."

"You are?" Crystal asked, pleased. "You see how really friendly we could have been."

"Here, put all the cream on the strawberries; there probably won't be much of it where you're going."

Crystal watched Sheridan dishing out the cream. "I've never seen you so happy, Sherry. Damn it, that's just what I don't understand. I mean neither of you ever seemed to me to be having a good time together . . . !"

"Who are you talking about?"

"You and Mrs. Markham."

"Describe the lady: I've forgotten her."

"I wouldn't be surprised if you had. Why, toward the end there on the island, I was with her more than you were. She probably told you how I asked her to go to Africa with me?"

"Matter of fact she did," Sheridan replied, smiling. "But let's get on with planning that trip of yours." However, he remembered his clothes rolled up in a heap on the bathroom floor of the *pensione*: he would have to return to the island anyway, wouldn't he, to get his things? For the moment he was depressed that he had left them there. Had he done so, he wondered, because he had not really wanted to leave, had known he would want to go back? A way out? Probably. Now he knew where he was going, though; certainly he knew what he wanted.

The Sea Wall

Crystal was looking rather self-conscious: "I'll bet the two of you had a good laugh over my asking her to come along."

"No. We so seldom laughed that I'd remember it."

"Then why the hell should you go away with her?" Crystal burst out. "You'll probably laugh at me, Sherry, but everything, since we met this morning, points toward us going to Africa together, and not you going off with Mrs. Markham!"

"What do you mean, Crystal?" Sheridan asked, hesitantly. "Why, I've been trying to tell you——"

"You don't have to tell me anything. I know all about it from Mrs. Markham. Why, she was so dreamy-dreamy about it, I thought for a minute she'd had too much sun."

"You forget that—that she's not young."

"I'm sorry I brought it up, Sherry. Shall we forget it? Look, while I take a shower, why don't you order more wine?"

Sheridan did so. He put down the telephone in a daze. Why hadn't she told him? Of course that's what she had wanted; it's what both of us wanted! He went to the bathroom and gathered up his clothes and dressed.

"Where do you and Mrs. Markham plan to go together anyway, Sherry?"

"Oh," Sheridan cried, overcome with gratitude, "maybe Africa."

"Then we'll see each other!" He came out in a towel; watched Sheridan pour the wine. Then he frowned and shook his head. "I feel I could begin all over again, don't you, Sherry? Martinis, then lunch, wine, shower, wine, and back again, and on and on till—— Oh, it has been neat! I only wish you could stay in Naples till I leave. Damn it, I'll bet by then you'd have convinced me about Spain."

"Did Mrs. Markham," Sheridan carefully asked, "speak to you often about our trip?"

"Just once, and you could have knocked me over with a feather. Which reminds me, I think I'll take a snooze." He got into bed, looking all the while slyly at Sheridan. "What are you thinking about, Sherry?"

"Oh, nothing. Maybe I'll take a walk."

Crystal broke into a laugh. "Leaving?" he asked, with mock surprise.

"Yes. I—I've just thought of something."

"Something I said?"

"Yes."

"Man, oh man!" Crystal rolled about on the bed giggling. "What a pair! She never told you, I knew it. Pour me some wine, and hurry on down to that boat. You don't even have to pay the bill, Sherry," he said, taking the glass. "I feel as rich, and drunk, and sentimental as my old man when he was nicest. Here's to you, Pop," Crystal shouted, holding

high over his head the wine. "Wish your little boy luck—
because he's a-seein' the world!"

Sheridan paid the bill and took a taxi to the dock. The
boat had just left. There would not be another until tomorrow morning. He stood for a good while looking at the
water. She would not want him anyway now, would she?
It had been the thought of the trip, the possibility of travel,
that had made him forget the fact that with Mrs. Markham
nothing was now possible.

Hoping this one would work, Sheridan grabbed at his
third hunch of the day. His first hunch had been to go off
to Africa with Crystal; his second, to return to the island;
now, taking a taxi to the railroad station, he used up his
last hunch in the purchase of a first-class ticket to Rome.
The ticket-seller went about getting the ticket, then stopped
and stared somewhat sinisterly over Sheridan's shoulder:
there was no one else waiting. "It's raining in Rome," he
said then. "Do you know how I know that? Well," the
ticket-seller continued, "my sister always calls me from
Rome when it rains. She just picks up the phone when she
feels the rain coming on, and calls me regardless of cost.
We are very close."

Mrs. Markham stepped out in the late afternoon. The
Signora Morabido, who had advised broth, *pochettino di*

broda al letto, was consoled only by the fact that their guest carried an umbrella. Buried in its scalloped shadow, Mrs. Markham was soon discovered by Haller. "I took you for a picnicker," she said, noting that the flowers were gone, the grass scorched: the path by the cliff, though altogether changed, was still lovely. Haller sketched a family in a boat. "I don't see them," Mrs. Markham commented quietly, and then she did, for they appeared chattering from behind a rock. The welt on her forehead, now famous throughout town, was visible to Haller. What really happened? he wondered. "Do you come here often, Mrs. Markham?" Mrs. Markham waved him to be still. "Go on with your work," she said, stepping off the path.

Palely attired in a lavender-colored silk suit, surmounted strictly by her umbrella, she looked, to Haller, like a Visitor to the Holy Land. Smiling, he gathered up his pencils. "Ah, so you've stopped," Mrs. Markham said, coming back to him. "Were you going to anyway?"

She accepted his invitation to cocktails—asking, as soon as she arrived at the house, hadn't there been flowers outside? "Wisteria, yes," Billy replied, laughing, "but it doesn't last forever." Did Mrs. Markham know they'd bought the house?

She drifted from room to room asking questions—"And these things, are they yours?"—but not listening to the answers. "Where we first met," she told Haller in the kitchen. "Yet," she laughed, "I've never believed in your first name."

"Well," said Billy, "it's what his father's supposed to have said when Haller was born: 'Hallelujah!' But most of us think it's what Haller himself says whenever he looks in the glass."

"How rude I was about your leaves, Billy," said Mrs. Markham.

"This," Billy told her, passing a doll bride in a bell jar on their way upstairs, "is ours, and that is, and the bed, and the marble-top table's ours."

Mrs. Markham wondered if she might hear some music. "I remember not hearing it at your party." She sat down for the first time. "You see, you only played it after we left." Startling her, a light came on sudden as a broken egg. "We must have forgotten it last night," Billy explained. "There was such a mix-up—about lights."

"Where," she asked, "do you think Sheridan's gone to?"

"We thought Rome, didn't we, Billy. They say he's left his stuff."

"His luggage . . . ?"

Billy's choice of music was unfortunate; he, at least, felt the Ravel concerto made their guest *look* crazy: "Matter of fact, Mrs. Markham, your suit's the color of wisteria."

"Corvo," she explained. "And Crystal"—she smiled—

"bought a beret . . . ! Of course we all know he quite possibly would leave those things for months."

"Or forever!" Billy was horrified she might wait for Sheridan to come back.

"But perhaps not," said Haller, hoping she would.

Mrs. Markham put down her glass and rose, looking about her for her umbrella. "I haven't listened much, have I? It was piano, wasn't it? Lovely."

"You can come again," Billy told her generously.

"Not unless it would be tomorrow," said Mrs. Markham.

"Of course tomorrow. Come for dinner. But why *only* tomorrow?"

"My last day, tomorrow. You see, I must be getting home. To America. Now, may I have my umbrella?"

A sense of peace enveloped Sheridan as he let himself into the foyer of the apartment he had once shared with Cooper. A purple-and-red glass lantern cast a mauve-colored light over the backs of his hands and over his face. He sat down quietly by the door, and when he did so his true feeling, leaving him unconstricted and free, fell from him: he was glad to be back. Cooper read aloud to someone in the adjoining room. All was familiar, easy, yet nothing of it could ever be attained honestly by him again. The fire flowers, Sheridan thought, smiling, and the rug lies thick, and the chair waits, but it is a world of things—not persons. He had returned from an experience which had all unawares so heightened his sense of life that it allowed him only the most melancholy hope of ever doing again what he had done before. I've come, he thought, to get my things. Your things? he asked himself. Aren't they just an excuse to get back? And now that you don't want to get back, and see you can't, you no longer need it. I was only going to be a minute, but now, he told himself as he stood up, put his hand silently on the door and opened it, I won't even be that: because I've a friend waiting at the bottom of the hill. . . .

The voice continued as he went out, sowing word after word in the silence. Yet as soon as he had gone it stopped. For a long time afterwards Cooper sat silently hunched over his table. Like many people involved seriously in the solitary task of composition, he was frequently visited by a teasing sense of loss, of isolation, a sense that while attempting to create a reality in art, the other reality, life in the streets—the immediate look of the Bridge of Angels in the rain—would have passed him by.

Also, it was not his love of writing, but a love of gadgets, that compelled him to dictate this novel. It was a torture, for rarely did Cooper fail to note his fingers moving, while he worked, as though they held a pen. This would pass, he thought; the intruding thunder and lightning of the storm would pass, too, over Rome and take with it the beguiling sound of the rain. Yet the rain fell, and falling, called to him. He had once had a relative dear to him, but now long gone, who, wearing a rubber cape, would leave his house and parrots in Brooklyn Heights and come ferrying across the river in the rain. "For it's the rain," he used to say, putting aside his light-reflecting garment, "that's called me out." Once in secret he had taken Cooper to Philadelphia to see Alla Nazimova play Mrs. Alving. After the perform-ance they traveled backstage, for the uncle was a singularly curious and restless soul. "May I, madam," Cooper always remembered him saying to the great actress, she in her shawl, he in his rubber cape, "present my nephew?" Na-zimova raised her expressive hands in a gesture of dismayed pleasure: "All the way from Brooklyn in this rain!"

Now, with the passing of years, the unfolding of the shyly shaded heart of youth, Cooper had come to consider this one way of his incomparable relative's his way too. So pushing back his dictating mechanism, the chair, and even the table a bit, the young man took his coat and descended into the city.

How indifferent the rain was that night, Sheridan, of the two, would know best. Through it he watched cats in a moat below street level behind the Pantheon, where there once had been an ancient bath. The cats hugged the drier side of broken columns, and blinked orientally into the blue, wet air.

"Are you watching them too?" a voice beside Sheridan asked. "I've been whistling at you for minutes, Sherry," said Mrs. Christophe, for it was she. "Now give me my reward, and I'll tell you how I got here."

"How did you get here, Chris?" he asked, kissing her. "But anyway I'm glad. Where's your husband?"

"I'm afraid," Mrs. Christophe replied simply, "that Chris has left me."

"What unreal things people do."

"Like whistling, you mean?" She put her hands to her face, and stood thus for minutes pressed against him. "Don't ever whistle in the rain, Sherry; it doesn't carry. I've been walking for hours, have you? But nobody listens; even the air, so busy getting washed and dressed, reflects my unemployment."

"The cats, then?"

"Yes, maybe the Caesar, Emperor cats would listen; and those with smaller heads, who must have once been cardinals."

"No saints?"

"I hadn't thought. My people were Quakers, and so I have no right to think of saints, or tears, or an audience with the Pope."

"The rain's stopped."

Friends and Vague Lovers

Silently the Pantheon's cats awakened and made arches of their backs as the moon, three-quarters old, bared itself in a nest of operatic clouds. Over the shivering streets people emerged to walk from arches and cafés; while boys encircled puddles like reeds conspiratorially murmuring of the storm that had passed over Rome like a circus parade. Batons of lightning speared distant clouds, but those above rolled on their backs in the brilliant mottled pasture of the moon.

Then Mrs. Christophe told her story:

"All we've ever had has cracked up since Europe; from Cherbourg on, I suppose, Chris felt green again; it was most crushing to me, my dear, the sense he gave me of the things he'd missed. I'd always been a bit apologetic for having married him, anyway. The strange thing was that Chris, even as far as Venice, kept reminding me that we must be getting home. He was frightened. What gave him courage was my shouting for such attention as I've never asked for in my life. Suddenly I was alone; afraid ever to hear the word 'we' used again. The light he'd begun to see in Cherbourg turned very bright in Venice. It told him to go now, or forever hold his peace; told him, one imagines, that he was forty, and probably would not get the chance again. Well, he took it."

Sheridan turned away.

"Don't you dare do that, you bastard!" Mrs. Christophe cried.

"Do what? What more can I do than I've done?"

"Everything by standing here with me."

But that, Sheridan felt, was just what he could not do. He could not listen to her, feel sorry for her; she made his own predicament loud to him.

"I'm catching a train to Naples, Chris."

"You're not catching a goddamned thing. You're locked out, and you know it, Sherry."

"Speak for yourself, my little wet friend."

"I've never been able to do that, Sherry," Mrs. Christophe replied. "It's you now I've got in my boat."

"Not quite. My way's by train, and alone. It's wretched of me, Chris, but I just can't stand you at this stage, and I don't believe you can stand me either. We'd hate each other in an hour."

The sudden projection of the two of them together somewhere like castaways, their intimacy heightened and concentrated within the closed doors of some hotel, made Sheridan certain he would have to get a train if only to get rid of her. Actually, however, he used Mrs. Christophe to make himself do quickly what he wanted to do most: get back to the island to Mrs. Markham.

Shrugging her little shoulders, Mrs. Christophe laughed.

"**Oh my dear,**" she bravely cried, "I'll get on. I took you for something you've probably never been to anybody, a possible companion. When I whistled I must have thought that we'd fit into each other's sorrows—a kind of Topsy and Eva version of Duse and Isadora, both of them sad and out of work; Duse trailing classical rags through the sand; Isadora endlessly consoling her about that little rat, D'Annunzio. How bad they must have been for each other. You're quite right. Shall we go?"

At the station, which smelled damply of cement, Mrs. Christophe gathered a stack of picture magazines from a mobile rack which she claimed entranced her. "Take them, Sherry, and forgive me my confession. Am I awfully wet-looking? Horrible? And my nose?"

"You're fine," said Sheridan, kissing her good-by.

"Of course I am. Someday I'll paint you a picture—a cat's-eye view of us in very blue rain outside the Pantheon. It was the Pantheon, wasn't it?"

The car moved; the station sprang open in an instant, all noise and commotion as car after car sped by. The train rushed away leaving an abyss of silence, a sprinkling of stop-and-go lights, smoke.

No light burned in Mrs. Markham's room; the ribs of her shutters were open and dark, but the shutters themselves were closed. The wharf was deserted and silent as failure; not a soul stirred in the piazza. Yet from the lighted café sounded the song of a flute. Sheridan, stepping swiftly between the tied-back bamboo and bead curtain, was greeted first by the flute player, a boy, who alone kept the eldest sister company.

"You are tired, Signor Sherry?" the eldest sister asked. Her voice clung to the air like the sound of a guitar.

"No, I am not tired, thank you, Signora," Sheridan replied. "I have been to Rome. I've returned to get my belongings, and pay my bills."

The eldest sister took up her cardboard fan, which she plied for a moment fretfully. "And then?"

"Oh, then?" he shrugged, "I suppose I will leave."

She seated herself urbanely before a plate of cold cuts.

"Who is he, Signora?" Sheridan inquired of the flute player.

"God only knows; he says I knew his father; the police probably want him too."

The boy's sun-hardened face brightened.

"Shall I give him something?" Sheridan asked.

The eldest sister snorted, and stomped out her cigarette. "The police, I say, are excited and happy. They say there was a struggle between you and the Signora Markham. Give him what you like!"

"How a struggle? I'm fascinated."

"So are the police: they will be difficult to disappoint. They have notified Rome, and your friend there. Why did you strike her on the head?"

"I didn't."

"So you were not there?"

"Yes, I was certainly there."

"And the glass?"

"I threw it."

Furious with Sheridan, the eldest sister turned on the flute player: "Stop it, you!" Regretting her rudeness, she then thoughtfully traced her name on the table with the handle of her fan. "Who knows," she smiled, "maybe I did know his father. Ayee!" She laughed, turning on the boy. "And suppose I did? Suppose I should keep you with me as a comfort? Would you then blow stars into my trees outside as you do now? Or would you just lazily grow up? Oh, play again, but do it softly." Within the sudden dome of music, which for a moment seemed to whirl the café around with it, the Signora came swiftly to the delicious, wicked point: "You perhaps gave her too much love; she is not young."

"Oh God, no."

"Not old?"

"No, Signora, I mean not lovers."

"Not lovers!"

"Of course not."

"Mother of God," the eldest sister laughed—simply fell all to pieces laughing, "then it is not serious. Oh, let us forget it, and you tell me about Rome."

"But afterwards I must go."

"It is too late to get into the *pensione*."

Sheridan showed her the key which he had never returned to the proprietor Morabido. "And my friend, Signora," he cautiously inquired, "is she still there?"

"She is," the Signora replied, laughing again. "But before you return to her to quarrel again, tell me of what interests me most. Tell me of Rome."

"Well, first of all it was raining . . . !"

The eldest sister's fan stood still with amazed interest. She got up and undid the bamboo and bead curtain which, clashing closed, startled the boy. "Tell me," she murmured, "of how it appears in the rain, my little Northerner's beloved city?" She settled herself down beside Sheridan with folded arms. "Now," she whispered, tilting her head, closing her eyes, "now."

Mrs. Markham arrived at Helion's wearing a traveling hat consisting of hundreds of meticulously pressed feathers of the darkest green. As a somewhat too strident reminder of her departure it was a success. Remembering what little of the concerto she had heard yesterday, she asked Billy if she might not now hear all of it, and then she would go. She listened almost attentively. There had been lobster, and white wine, and an enormous green salad, and now it was late. "Send us a card," said Billy. "Of what—Boston?" Mrs. Markham replied; and, such as it was, it was their farewell.

Arriving back at the *pensione,* Mrs. Markham went immediately to bed and was awakened only once during the night: she did not believe what she had heard, sounds of somebody in the next room. Drawing up the sheet, she frowned and dozed off again, though not for long: there was the boat whistle, then tea, then she herself was up, dressed again, and standing rather dazed on the balcony.

"So it was you," she said across to him. "You've come back after all." She touched her hat, wondering, quizzically, what he thought of her in it. Then she smiled, nodded, she supposed, good-by, and went in.

She threw one swift, hard look around the room, took up the coat which had been Jonathan's, slipped it about her shoulders, and left. Descending the stairs, she noted his luggage in the morning light, his air of nervousness, or was it of decision? She thought that it was rather like— Despite the Morabidos, and despite Antonia, it was precisely like her last morning with Jonathan.

[236]

The Sea Wall

"Where in the world are *you* bound for, Sheridan?" she coldly asked. "You've only just arrived. At any rate we can travel as far as Naples together, can't we?"

They shook hands with the Morabidos and Antonia, then hurried down through the sunlight to the wharf. As Mrs. Markham stepped into the crowded rowboat, her topcoat was lifted from her shoulders: "Oh, thank you, Sheridan. Why I wear it in this heat I simply don't know." He sat down beside her, the coat folded over his lap. The boat cut through the bright waves toward the nodding vessel. Mrs. Markham raised her arm to Antonia, who waved from the balcony. "I had thought maybe Rome," she said, musingly, "but now no. I'd like, I think, Sheridan, to go very far north, yet still remain inland. Can we do that?" There was but the faintest hint in her voice that she had just risked all; and won. "Wave to the child, Sheridan."

La Méditerranée's whistle rose like an obelisk of sound, then fell, then rose again as around the Americans various women blessed themselves in preparation for this journey.